UMBRATE

This book is a work of fiction. Any reference to real events, people, or places are used fictitiously. Other names, characters, places and incidents are the products of the author's imagination. Any resemblance to actual events, locales, or persons; living or dead, is entirely coincidental.

UMBRATE

A.D JONES

For my parents,
The heroes of my story.

PROLOGUE

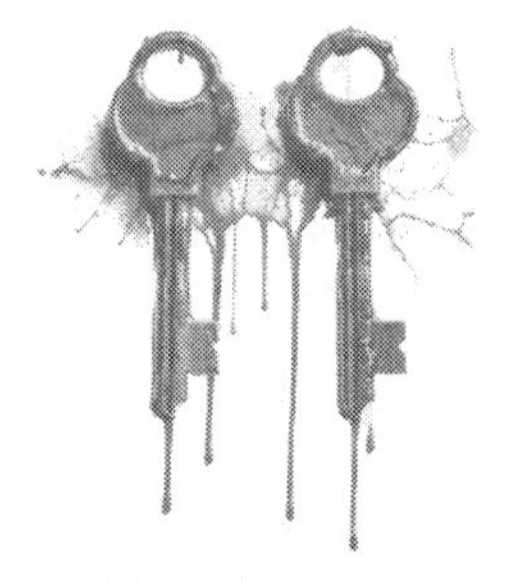

Centuries ago…

The wheels of the wagon rolled across the dirt path, led by a pair of chestnut brown horses. The placid blue hues of the sky had ebbed to a dismal grey, edged with autumn-leaf-orange.

The two riders seated up front watched as the tree line on each side of the road began to slowly close ranks and arch above the trail, spindly fingers tentatively attempting to touch across the gap.

Gripping the leather straps tighter, the stout bearded man at the reins turned to face his travelling companion, a man of slight build with a tight angular face and dark, shoulder-length hair. He noticed for the first time that his breath was becoming visible in the increasing cold.

"This'll be it, ya know. The next couple of hours are gonna be the hairy ones fer sure," he said.

"Floric, there's a term we use where I come from, Famous last words. I swear if you've just invoked them, the beasts out here will be the last of your problems," said Peter, with a wry smirk.

"Alls I'm saying is be alert, you've better eyes than me."

They carried on along their journey for the better part of two hours, Floric periodically glancing down at the rune carved hammer at his feet, occasionally gripping the leather wrapped handle like a parent squeezing a child's hand for reassurance.

As the dark, and cold closed in around them they came to a forking of the road, a large boulder in the middle of the path acting as a huge stone divider. It appeared, to their viewpoint, that the road reconnected on the other side and carried on, making either left or right a viable option.

Peter turned and eyed Floric with a look of trepidation and suspicion. The dwarf met his gaze, gave a quick nod, and looked back to the road, giving the reins a sharp tug as they moved forward.

Slowly following the road to the right, they moved along finding themselves now on a narrower path, only seven or eight feet of space either side of the cart, sandwiching them between the rock face and the forest to their right.

An immediate drop in temperature was their first warning. The darkness began to close in around them and from up ahead they saw shadows appearing from behind the far end of the boulder they were to pass.

The horses reared up in panic as the shadows came into view. Not the shadows of people, but the shadows themselves.

Each standing at around six feet tall, seven figures stepped into view. In the approximation of human form, their entire bodies were black as obsidian so dark that bright white highlights reflecting from the moon accented their features. Varying attempts at hair took the form of smooth curls or spikes rising and waving from their heads like black flames; the ends of their fingers looked like smooth shadowed talons.

"Ambush!" shouted Floric, as he reached for his warhammer and jumped down from the wagon, bracing for attack.

Peter, in unison had leapt from his side of the wagon and drew a pair of pointed Stiletto daggers from his waist, dropping to a crouch, feet spread wide, poised, and ready.

Without hesitation, the shadow creatures darted forward and began to close the gap on the wagon, arms outstretched, claws gleaming sharp in the moonlight, sounding off in unison with a noise that somehow managed to be both a hiss and yet preternaturally low and gravelly.

A high whirring sound passed between them, followed by a crack akin to the splitting of wood as Floric and Peter watched an arrow sink firmly into the shoulder of the nearest shadow.

"Perhaps a tad more warning next time?" came the voice of Vandra, now stood where they'd sat only moments ago, bow in hand. Her sandy blonde hair tied back into an intricate braid, revealed her pointed ears. A delicate V-shaped tattoo ran from the bridge of her nose and up to her hairline.

Coming out from the wagon behind her stood Scarlett, her long auburn hair flowing in the wind. Her bow lifted as she began to take aim, flanked by the muscular dark-haired form of Cal, his wooden buckler and an iron sword raised ready, stepping carefully over the seat in front.

The first shadow creature closed the gap and dove at Peter, arms crossing in a double slashing motion. He deftly dodged back and swung upwards with his fist sending the creatures left arm into the air as he followed up by driving the dagger directly into its armpit, the quickest way to reach the heart.

It let out a guttural scream and leapt back, but to Peters dismay, regrouped and pounced forward again slashing across his face with its right claw.

The pain was sharp and intensely cold, and the four slashes felt like barbs of ice tearing into his flesh. Readying himself for another swing he crouched low and raised his daggers.

A shadow fell across his right side, and he turned to face a second attacker as he saw instead, the familiar form of Cal fly past him and onto the creature, knocking it to the ground.

Briefly touching his face to check the damage, he stepped forward to help his friend, now tussling with the creature on the ground.

Apparently having the upper hand, Cal kneeled on the fallen creature, raised himself up and let out a bestial roar as he readied himself to plunge his sword into the fallen shadow.

Thick black shards shot out the back of Cal's skull as Peter watched in horror as the creature had forced its hand up through Cal's throat and into his head. The wet crunching sound sickened him to his core as he watched Cal's body go limp, still elevated on the protruding arm like a lifeless puppet.

On the other side of the wagon a second arrow found its mark in the chest of the creature moving towards Floric. He pushed forward to meet the attacker and with a low swing of his hammer caught its left knee, dropping it to a kneel as its leg buckled under the sickening crack. With it brought down to his height, Floric seized the opportunity and swung his hammer with all his strength, crushing its skull under the mighty blow.

Shaking off the ache he felt reverberating up through his arms and shoulders, he found his composure and flung himself shoulder-first into the nearest enemy as they charged towards the wagon.

The scent of fresh blood was in the air as the incessant beating of his heart and the blood-curdling scream from behind him rang in his ears.

Scarlett had evidently seen what happened to Cal.

Peter stared in fear at the limp form of his friend in front of him. He pounced forward at the creature as it cast off the corpse of his friend and his blades finished the job Cal had started, a wicked cross slash at the monster's throat, slicing so deep the head was practically severed from its body.

Surveying the area, he saw Floric rush the oncoming attack and charged forward to help flank from the left.

Despite the pincer defence, two of the creatures had made it through and Peter could see that Vandra had dropped her bow and drawn a bronzed shortsword, while Scarlett readied another arrow by her side.

He stabbed furiously at the nearest creature, trading sloppy swings as its claws returned the same energy, both giving and receiving a series of cuts and slashes in turn.

Stealing a quick glance across the battlefield he watched as Floric swung his hammer directly into the stomach of his foe dealing massive injury, but finding the hammer now lodged in its form.

Filled with both panic and bloodlust, he feinted a swing and lurched forward driving both daggers into the creature's chest at the collarbones in a tapered stab. Bracing himself, he pulled up and rotated outwards with the blades, carving open its throat.

Not giving himself chance to breathe, Peter rushed to Floric's aid, as he was now locked in battle with two enemies, his right arm grappled as the hammer damaged foe dove forward and raked its claws down his chest, shredding his armour and opening up the flesh beneath.

An arrow hit the creature's chest as Peter turned and saw the horses fleeing at speed, with Scarlett now dropping her bow, knife in hand as she and Vandra were pushed back into retreat as the wagon was boarded.

Wasting no time, Peter leapt onto the creature and buried his left dagger into its back as he grabbed the shaft of the arrow with his other hand. Using the momentum gained he pulled it back and flung it round, sending them both rolling across the ground, dislodging Floric's hammer in the process.

Scrambling to his knees, he again flung himself onto it and began stabbing furiously at the fallen creature until its angry hissing ceased and it fell limp under his body.

Screams from the wagon began to fill the air, sending a cold shiver up his spine as he turned to see Floric facing him, arm wrenched up towards his back, the glaring enemy behind him.

The sickening wet sound of flesh tearing elevated Peters stomach as the cartilage was ripped from Floric's throat by a clawed hand.

As his body was released and began to fall, Peter threw his remaining dagger forward, his aim true, and it stuck with a *thunk* into the eye of the creature, sending it falling backwards to the ground.

After rushing to retrieve the dagger, Peter moved to Floric. The blood was still warm on his hands, but he was beyond saving and with no time to spare Peter burst into a sprint towards the wagon.

Leaping up onto the drivers' seat, he peered into the wagon to see a single creature moving towards Vandra as she shuffled backwards, the soles of her boots slipping on the wagons floor as she scuffled into a corner.

The women had taken out one of the creatures, and its body lay motionless on top of Scarlett. Up close, Peter could see the deep lacerations covering Scarlett's face and body. Both were seemingly dead.

Peter lunged into the wagon as the creature fell on Vandra. Her cries were sharp but short, and once again he buried his blade into the creature's back.

It twisted around fast, sending Peter flying in the close quarters of the wagon, dagger still lodged between its shoulder blades.

As he landed, the back of his head caught the corner of a large trunk, sending a shockwave of pain through him.

His vision started to blur as he saw the creature move forward with its hands raised, revealing a vicious smile of black jagged teeth, Vandra's blood and flesh still clinging to its claws.

With a guttural roar it fell on Peter and started to rip and tear at his flesh like a crazed animal.

Sharp pain and warmth filled his body as slash upon slash sent blood flying into the air. All he could do was raise his arms in defence of the onslaught of blows.

Famous last words, he thought, as searing pain flowed through him, and his body began to involuntarily shiver as his vision faded to black.

CHAPTER ONE

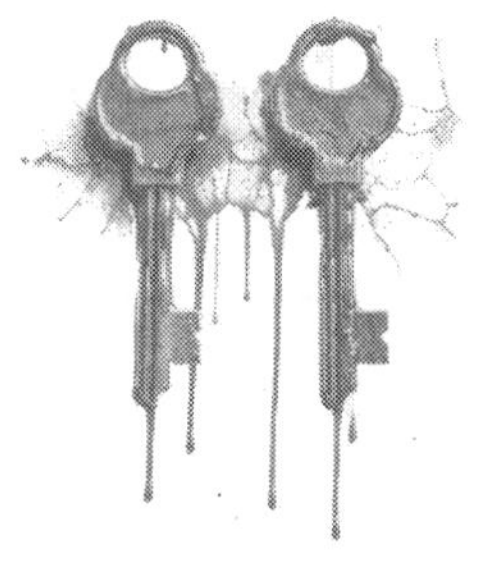

Now

A brilliant white light filled the bedroom, cascading across the wall from east to west as the gentle thrum of a car's engine passed outside, like a brief visit from an antiquated lighthouse, before plunging the room back into darkness.

Vanic sat up in bed, disorientated and slightly groggy. The faint red glow from the television's standby light lit up like a pinprick portal to hell.

He threw back the covers and winced at the pain in his side. Blood seeped through the white cotton dressings that covered his injuries.

Figuring he'd managed to open up the cuts in his sleep, and that this had woken him, he chewed the acrid taste out of his mouth. He turned to look at the alarm, past the sleeping form of Roma, her pale shoulder practically aglow in the night against her flowing dark hair.

Four Thirty-seven.

Far too early. He still couldn't get to grips with the shift to his sleeping pattern when outside of his scheduled work rota, but he had absolutely earned the few days leave to recover from his injuries.

He leaned over and laid a gentle kiss on the bare shoulder, her skin cool and oddly refreshing, goose-bumped against his lips before rolling over and burying his face into the pillows and pulling the sheet up to his chin, settling back into slumber.

FRESH COFFEE IN HAND, VANIC WALKED UP TO THE DOORS OF the station, pausing to let two uniformed officers exit, a nod and swift sip of his drink as they passed.

Stepping inside, the overpowering smell of bleach filled his nostrils and the harsh brightness of the overhead fluorescents lit up the whitewashed walls. A moody looking teen with lank black hair, faded heavy metal t-shirt and jeans ripped at the knee, eyed him from the bench as he approached the front desk.

"Still haven't come to terms with the concept of a day off then?" said the woman at the desk, cropped blonde hair swept to one side, her regulation pale blue shirt starched and pristine.

"I just have a few bits to get in order for Friday, Clara, I swear. You can chase me if I'm not walking my ass out of here in half an hour," Van said as he raised his hands in mock surrender.

"Yeah, yeah. Heads up, Visp is in today, so play nice."

"Me? Always," Van pressed a hand on his chest as he walked backwards through the door behind her.

As he passed along the rows of empty desks, Vanic was reminded of the eeriness in how quiet the station was during the daytime. He wasn't sure why, but it always bothered him and was glad when he finally arrived at his desk.

Placing down his coffee, he pulled out his chair and took a seat before he powered up the computer, watched the screen blinking to life, and noticed a white envelope placed neatly under his keyboard.

Detective Bradley,

Many thanks for your work at City Hall recently. Your swift actions helped prevent major incident and the potential loss of life. I greatly appreciate all the hard work you, and everyone there at the precinct, do and would like to offer a little thanks at this time.

Please find enclosed Three tickets for the Quarterstone Zoo for the coming week, including tickets for the opening performance of the new Vilgore exhibit and show. I am told its quite something. It is just a small token of my, and the city's appreciation.

Should the Tuesday be less than ideal (chosen purely to coincide with the debut Vilgore show), or three tickets not be sufficient, please contact my secretary on the number below and we shall have that rectified.

Yours thankfully

Terence Farnham, Mayor

Inside the envelope were six small tickets, three purple with metallic gold lettering and three smaller white show tickets. How odd. He would consider this some sort of bizarre bribe, were it not an afterthought.

Vanic let his mind wander and quickly found himself back inside the offices of City Hall, the pain in his side a fresh reminder of the attack. He could vividly recall the memory of rolling through broken glass and debris, fighting for his life. The intense burning of the claw marks on his body and the blood running freely as he struggled with his attacker. The explosive sound of pistol shots still bounced around his head as he again saw the life leave the eyes of the umbral man before him. Dead by his hand.

A cold shiver ran down his spine before he folded the tickets back into the envelope and readied himself to deal with some emails when his phone started to vibrate in his pocket. *What now?*

Taking out his phone with a sigh, he glanced at the screen.

Josh. His closest friend for as long as he could remember.

"Hello?"

"Just checking you're not sat thinking of ways to blow me off."

"Only if you buy me enough drinks." Juvenile, but it was an ongoing joke between them.

"Ha. Ha." His voice clearly slow and robotic, to show he was less than impressed. "Pina Colada's then. So, we're still good for eight?"

He paused for a second and ran a quick mental scan of possible ways he could get out of it, before resigning himself.

"Yeah, eight's fine. Meet you at Queezy's?"

"The same Queezy's that's been closed for over a year? Yeah, that's fine, we'll sort where we're going from there. Right, speak to you soon."

It was starting to get dark by the time he'd left the station, and Clara's shit-eating grin beamed at him as he walked past her. He playfully flipped her the bird over his shoulder as he made his way out of the building and towards the subway.

He didn't have to wait long for the train and thankfully it was relatively quiet on the platform. There was maybe twenty or so people on each side. Set up against the wall that divided the stairs leading down to the platform, a young girl busked with her guitar, one chunky platformed boot resting on her amp. She wore a grey vest top and black denim shorts with skeleton-bone tights underneath. Her cascading purple dreadlocks flowed like jungle vines down her body, allowing just the slightest peek of her pointed ears sticking through. He had to admit, she was pretty good.

The train arrived after a few minutes and everyone formed a polite queue at the doors, allowing the alighting commuters to exit the train first before stepping on.

The journey was only a short ride into the city, but he found a seat with ease, settling down to people watch. Even though he was off duty, the sense that people were eyeing him warily was always present. The awkward shifting of eyes avoiding contact all the while trying not to look guilty, even without having done anything wrong.

Making excellent time, he left the subway and marched up the high street. The stores starting to show signs of closing and people milled about with their shopping bags of likely unnecessary purchases.

He arrived at Queezy's right on time to find Josh already waiting, leaning against the dark window of the now closed bar. Dressed in a grey sweatshirt with embroidered '*Go Town*' gym logo, khaki chino trousers and some unnecessarily loud trainers, he looked sufficiently out of place. Something his lanky frame in no way helped.

"So, shall we find ourselves a table? Or shall we perhaps head to a more functioning venue?" Josh said with a grin.

"Alright, it's been a while. I get it. It's on you to figure out where we're going then."

"Ha! There's a new place that's supposed to be decent, we can give that a try and go from there." Josh moved forward and playfully shoulder checked Vanic as they set off up the street.

They heard the music before they even laid eyes on the bar, a corner building with pink neon signs offering 'booze and tunes' and the '*Vortex Bar*' venue name across one side, in a logo that reminded Vanic of the over-the-top neon movies from his childhood.

A group of people were congregating outside the entrance smoking and, in the case of the women, dancing. The almost video game-like, synth music pulsing out into the Street.

Moving through the crowd, Vanic was about to step inside when he felt himself being pulled back by the shoulder. Josh let go and pointed to a smaller sign in the window beside the door.

"SUN DOWNERS NOT WELCOME"

"Maybe we should give this one a miss. Plus, it looks like they're all barely out of short pants in here anyway," Josh said, the distaste visible on his face.

"It's your rodeo, did you have a plan B?" Vanic said, trying not to show his indifference to the sign.

"Plan two. Plan B implies I only have twenty-six of them," Josh said with a smug grin. "Let's just head over to Lucio's for now and see where we go from there, yeah?"

Vanic rolled his eyes in an overly exaggerated gesture.

"Always trying to get me to the gay bars. Fine, but if I see you carrying one pina colada, I'm out!"

CHAPTER TWO

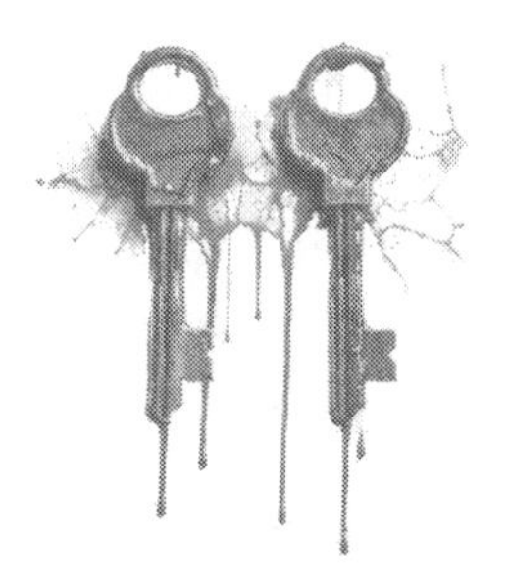

F. 7.

Artie Toomes punched the buttons and waited patiently as the machine came to life, the slow whirring sound emanating from it as the metal coil twisted and the golden wrapped candy bar snaked towards the glass. The almost slowing of time as he waited, practically expecting something to go wrong, was ended by the *Thunk* of the chocolate bar hitting the bottom of the vending machine.

After pulling open the drawer, he scooped up his prize and immediately tore it open and took a bite, the caramel and nougat blending perfectly with the chocolate coating.

Catching his reflection staring back at him, an almost walrus of a man, heavy set and round faced with thick brows and a bushy moustache that wouldn't look amiss on the end of a primary school paintbrush, his dirty blue overalls highlighting his middle-aged paunch. "Yeah yeah, well I didn't see you stopping me," he said to his reflection before checking his watch.

8.53.

While he had always made it a point of pride to never be late for anything, it doubly made sense when there was money involved, he thought to himself.

He paused for a moment to take in the plastic sealed poster set between the elevators, the new Valloresta brothers movie. The poster showing a beautiful elven woman sandwiched between a rugged human man and a twice as rugged dwarf, all in fighting stances to a backdrop of volcanos, explosions, and dragons. He enjoyed a fantasy film as much as the next person but preferred fast car chases and spy movies personally.

After making his way through the doors, he headed into the car park and towards the area he'd been told to meet last time, finishing up his treat and pocketing the wrapper.

After about ten minutes of waiting, periodically checking the brown envelope was indeed still nestled safely in his pocket, he heard a door clicking in the far distance of level three and grew tense. Less than a minute later he watched as, like a horror movie, the rows of strip lighting hanging from small chains on the ceiling began to extinguish one by one in sequence leading towards him.

Plunged into darkness, his initial thought was that you didn't realise how deafening the sound of those buzzing halogen lights were until they were suddenly silenced. The air around him plunged by a degree or two.

"Toomes, as punctual as ever I see. And with the documents I hope?" came a low, gravelly voice in the darkness.

Artie felt an immediate shiver run down his spine at the voice, and how it seemed to drag out the S as the end of his name.

"A..absolutely," he said as he reached into his pocket for the envelope before thrusting it out in front of him.

"Though I feel it's my duty to point out that these are clearly meant to be precautionary measures and shouldn't be considered something more nefarious." The irony of defending information he had stolen, was clearly lost on him.

"Oh really. You think the ability to lock down a mall's exits, and completely prevent the entire umbral populace from escaping is precautionary? Anyway, you needn't worry yourself. My plans for these don't involve anything as uncouth and boorish as a smear campaign. Nor as before, will they find any way to lead back to you. I am as always, a man of discretion."

Artie felt the envelope being pulled gently from his hand and replaced with another smaller yet fuller one. A further shiver ran over him at the cold momentary second of contact between them. Hearing the footsteps moving away, he remained rooted on the spot for what felt like an age before the lights began to fire up into life. The gentle hum returned with force before the clicking sound of the door in the distance repeated.

Now opening the envelope, he was greeted by the sight of the rows of bills stuffed inside. An easy payday. He secreted it into his pocket and headed back towards the elevators.

CHAPTER THREE

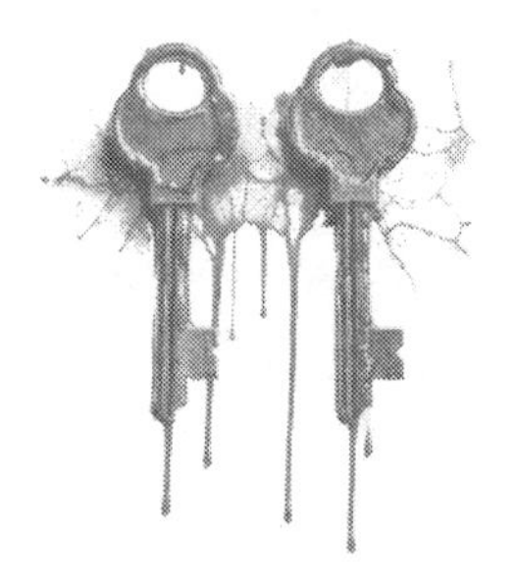

Josh stared at Vanic with a look of disbelief.

"So, you're saying this Visp guy saves people, and that annoys you?" he said with a grin.

"No." Vanic's eyes bulged. "This is my point. He does that job because he's not in any danger and yet it's like he's some big hero."

Josh still looked confused. "Look, you're going to have to explain this properly for me. Break it down."

Vanic downed the dregs of his beer and continued. "Ok, so he's an umbral right? And he wears an OTS."

"That's one of those hazmat looking suits with the mirror face mask yeah?" Josh interrupted.

"Outdoor travel suit, yeah," he continued. "So, he gets sent to dangerous assignments, Bomb disposal, for instance. His job is to go and assess the risks and defuse if possible. But my point is, there is no danger. If he finds himself in a situation that he can't stop, or something goes wrong: He just takes the helmet off and 'poof'…"

"The sun hits him, and he's gone,' Josh interjected again. 'You've got to admit though, that's smart."

"I'm not disputing that—"

Their conversation was cut short as a diminutive stout man with a round face the size of a dinner plate, approached their table with a tray of drinks. His bright red cheeks glowed like a slightly concerned adult cherub.

He reached up and placed their beers onto the table with a beaming grin, tucked the empty tray under his arm and turned away back towards the bar with a skip in his step.

"Don't you find it unsettling?" Vanic frowned. "He's Like some creepy angelic gargoyle."

"Man, you are on one tonight. Not every dwarf wants a beard, Van, and do you know how many times a day they need to shave?"

Vanic ran his finger up along the side of his glass, following a bead of amber liquid that was running down his pint. "Yeah ok, maybe you're right."

"Have you maybe considered the fact that you're perhaps a little racist?" Josh cocked an eyebrow at him.

"Come on, that's not fair, I just think their heads are too big for their bodies without the beard is all."

"Well, you seem to not like umbrals, and that's a pretty big sales point when it comes to racism,' said Josh "I'm just saying."

"Whoah!" Vanic screwed up his face. "It's not like that at all. I have no issues with them as a people, but I mean…" he paused to think about his response. "Ok, consider why a chicken is scared of a fox."

Josh took a long sip and frowned. "Because they're a threat? You're not helping your case here."

"No! Because that's what they deal with. I work the night shift. So, what I'm saying is, a good chunk of the criminals I deal with are in fact umbral. I suppose when you deal with that as a majority maybe I have taken on a slightly tainted world view. And let's not forget that it was an umbral man that recently came close to leaving my Son fatherless. But anyway, look at how people are, there must be a reason people are so hostile towards them."

Josh paused to take in their surroundings. Lucio's was one of the bigger bars in the area, and while it fell under the umbrella term of gay bar, it was in fact more of a safe place for just about anyone regardless of sexuality, gender, or species. As a result, this made for a successful establishment, always bursting with patrons, and tonight was no exception. A brief glance across the venue showed groups of humans, elves, dwarves and obsidian black umbrals were scattered in groups, both separate and intermixed, happily enjoying their night.

"A lack of understanding for the most part. People fear what they don't understand."

Vanic considered his words for a moment as Josh continued.

"I mean, they literally disappear in sunlight, and just reappear in the same place when it goes dark. They don't seem to get sick, or as far as we're aware, have internal organs the way we do. Yet they eat, drink, fuck, and age just like any other human or elf or whatever. I think ultimately, we're jealous."

"I don't know, I'm pretty partial to the feeling of the sun on my skin," Vanic said, knowing he sounded argumentative.

"Yeah? And ask someone with stage 4 skin cancer if they'd give up their holidays in the Xerathors to be healthy!"

Vanic chewed his lip. "Ok, I can see your point. But still, it's odd that it translates to prejudice."

Josh took another sip of his beer and stared at Vanic.

"Honestly, Van, it makes me wonder."

"Wonder what?" he said, his intrigue piqued.

"Well, how things could have been different. Let's say there weren't any umbrals. Now look around. I'm the blackest person here."

Vanic choked on his beer and tried to stop himself from spluttering. "What? You aren't even remotely black, you've lost me." He looked down at his own olive skin, only slightly lighter than Josh's. He'd never given either of their skin colors a second thought, except when he tanned a little in the summer. It made his black hair, athletic build and well-defined jaw stand out even more, and people would ask him sometimes if he had a tropical heritage.

"No, but I'm saying comparatively. It's the next best thing. Who's to say if it wasn't for umbrals taking the brunt of it, that my dark brown skin tone could have come under fire, you get me?"

"And you're saying I'm on one tonight! You're being ridiculous now, and this is getting heavy." He paused. "All I was saying is Visp is a dick! Anyway, it's your round."

CHAPTER FOUR

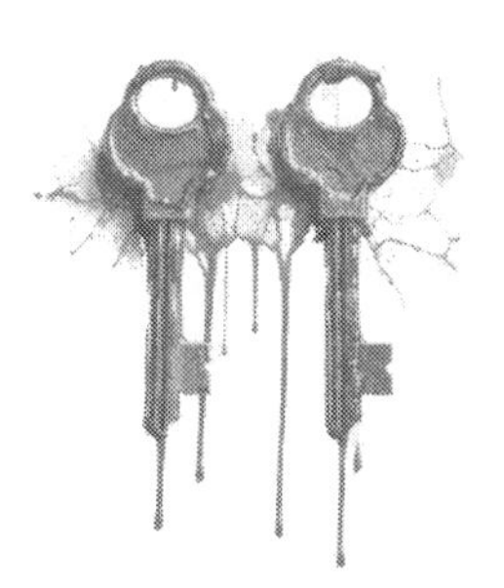

As had infuriatingly become the pattern, Vanic woke a minute before his alarm sounded. Flailing blindly, he reached for his phone on the dresser and quickly cancelled the alarm, which was always satisfying to do, knowing it had seconds to spare. Rolling out of bed, he stretched his arms skyward and felt the satisfying pops and cracks of the bones across his shoulders and back.

He caught sight of himself in the mirror briefly, his toned frame intermittently tarnished with various scars, before reaching for the joggers he'd melted out of the night before and stepping into them.

He headed down the stairs without adding a shirt. Pointless to wear one just to remove it again to shower after breakfast.

Roma sat cross legged on a chair in the lounge, intently focused on a bowl of cubed watermelon pieces. As he crossed the room, she smiled brightly at him.

"Mornafternoon" she quipped for the umpteenth time in their relationship. "There's coffee in the pot, pancakes on the counter and other breakfast stuffs in their true ingredient forms still in the refrigerator, but that's your problem."

Stepping in close, he placed two fingers under her chin and tilted her head up, lowered his face to meet hers, forehead to forehead. "You know, if you weren't so terribly hideous, you'd make someone a fantastic girlfriend." He planted a kiss on her lips.

"Sir, you flatter me. I am but a lowly dog faced woman," came her response. "Now go eat some pancakes before they go cold."

As Van stepped into the kitchen, the rich aroma of coffee filled his nostrils and the cool tiles against his bare feet refreshed him. Deciding against tackling anything more arduous, he opted to pile high a plate of pancakes and added a generous amount of syrup. After filling a mug of steaming coffee, he headed back to the lounge.

"So," he began. A fork-load of pancake entered his mouth and he absentmindedly masticated through his words. "Are you up for this Zoo thing with Noah, or are you working?"

"Working, sadly, but I think you're capable of having fun without me. If Sarah's free it might be nice for Noah to have a day with his mom and dad anyway." She levelled a weak smile his way.

He'd expected this to be the case, and wasn't overly disappointed by the confirmation, but was as always still blown away by how thoughtful and understanding she was. The TV shows and movies he'd grown up with didn't paint girlfriends to be so pleasant about a guy's ex-wife. She really was a keeper.

After his divorce, he'd tried the usual dating apps, but they were all hideously impersonal, and he soon decided that if he were to meet someone, it would have to be organically.

Vanic had met Roma through one of his biggest loves – coffee. She was a barista at his local morning drop-in, and they'd gradually began talking on his daily visits. Just short interactions at the counter to begin with, then when the decorative flair on his coffee cups transcended beyond his name to intricate little doodles, he decided to grow a pair and ask her out.

THE RAIN WAS LIGHT, BUT CONSISTENT AND HAD BEEN FALLing for over an hour. A black sedan idled at the curb, hidden in the shadows of the buildings on either side of the road. The stone apartment blocks had aged to a deep grey, and the walls were smeared with patches of mildew.

Lights flashed intermittently from the windows, as televisions broadcasted the evening news, tired sitcoms, or weekly soap dramas, adding an additional backdrop of gloom.

Inside the car, the driver and his passenger watched the wiper blades gently passing across the windshield in their slow hypnotic fashion, the rhythmic clicks and squeak of rubber on glass breaking the silence of the evening.

"I'm just saying we should have subs or take-out, or at least some deli sandwiches." The passenger was a man in his thirties with lank blonde hair, a large drooping nose and an overbite sporting huge front teeth. His look of disappointment perfectly suited his rat-like features.

"And I've told you twice already, that this is neither a cop show nor a stake-out," said Vanic, from his seat behind the wheel. "We're just waiting for everyone to get in place." He glanced at his watch and confirmed that they were still on schedule.

Ratface pondered this for a moment before continuing. "Well yeah ok, but I still think if you knew we were going to be sat waiting around all night, that I could have brought a snack." He began digging around in his trouser pockets with both hands before coming up with a half-finished, misshapen, and gods only knows how old, packet of gum.

Vanic shot him the swiftest look of disdain before returning his focus back to the windshield. His patience with officer Grady had been wearing thin from the second they'd pulled up here and he silently willed things to hurry up and move forward with tonight's sting, something that had been in the making for months.

As if answering his prayers, a rapping sounded from the right window of the car, and Vanic quickly hit the button to lower it as a bearded man in a long coat and dockers hat barely containing his dark damp locks leaned down, rain dripping from his nose.

"Everyone's in place and we're pretty much good to go on your call." He looked straight past Grady and addressed Vanic. "They know to expect me, so it should go as smoothly as planned, all things going well."

It didn't matter how many times they had worked together, Vanic was always greatly impressed with how entirely passable Sturridge was at playing the role of a vagrant or lowlife, whenever the need arose.

"Excellent. Get yourself into place and I'll radio everyone to get into position and signal you when we're ready. And be sure to get the hell out of the way asap."

The huge brick warehouse was set back from the streets through a web of railed and mesh fences that made up this industrial estate of warehouses and car garages. Many buildings on the estate appeared to be empty and long out of use, falling into total dilapidation and the garages, while still in use were dark and silent at this time in the evening. The lights coming from this building felt like an affront to their own secrecy. A single intimidating rusted metal door apparently served as the only entrance.

Officer Sturridge stood a few yards from the door, doing his best to look inconspicuous while he waited for everyone to get into place. He looked soaked to the bone, and Vanic couldn't tell if his shivers were from nerves or the cold.

They approached the building slowly, weapons drawn. Vanic took the lead with Grady to his left and six other officers brought up the rear in a two-by-two creep along the wall. The rest of the squad had been placed by the only presumed other exit to the building, ready for any potential runners. Vanic raised his open hand as he closed on Sturridge, to both signal his approach and stop the train of officers to his rear. He closed his hand into a fist to signal it was time and they started to quietly creep forward hugging the wall as Sturridge made his way to the door and banged on it four times with his fist.

Vanic's heart raced, and he could feel the familiar pulse in his temples as he froze in place. The metal grating on the door screeched across with a final sliding *thunk* of metal on metal in response to Sturridge's knocking. Vanic was too far away to hear the conversation in front of him, but he knew very well that Sturridge was a master of his art and would maintain a perfect volume as to not give away anything to the person on the other side of the door. Vanic braced himself against the wall, pistol gripped in both hands and aimed at the ground. A drip of sweat run down the back of his neck. After a minute or two of back and forth at the door, he heard the slide and click of the viewing hole again and Sturridge shot him a quick nod before taking a couple of steps back as the sound of bolts moving could be heard from within.

Vanic tensed, readying himself as the door flew open before him and he darted forward slamming into the man who'd stepped out, with the force of a quarterback and sending him into the back of the open door. Vanic stepped sideways into the building as Grady rushed forward, gun raised to stop the doorman in his tracks as the rest of the men followed behind him. Grady and Sturridge were now manning the exit, so Vanic moved forward with the six remaining officers into the depths of the building.

They moved silently down the corridor, guns raised, and Vanic hoped the commotion hadn't already alerted anyone else inside. He really wanted this to go smoothly for once. The corridor opened into a massive space with rail walkways around the perimeter, dropping twenty feet to the lower level into an inverted ziggurat, like a huge empty swimming pool. The lower level was filled with tables, workbenches and an abundance of chemistry or alchemical paraphernalia, as well as half a dozen men and women working away. Three men stood on the walkway ahead of them, two umbrals and what looked like a human male further down the corridor. Their presence was noticed immediately and the time for subtlety had passed. Vanic quickly gave order for two of the men to follow him as he raced towards the men in the corridor, leaving the remaining officers to secure the workers below.

Ahead of them, the two umbrals, one in a bright orange sweatshirt and camo trousers, the other in a simple white tee and black jeans, had seen them coming and sprinted down the walkway towards two doors at the back of the room, while the officers quickly attempted to close the gap. Risking no chance of being slowed down, the orange clad man shoved the obstructing human, who was still frozen in a presumed panic, over the side of the railing and Vanic was sadly just too far out of reach to attempt a rescue. He watched the man tumble over the side and heard his brief scream instantly silenced by the following thud.

Vanic carried on in pursuit of the fleeing criminals. At the end of the walkway stood a single wooden door to the left and a set of double doors straight ahead. Unsurprisingly, the fleeing men split up, orange sweatshirt carrying on through the doors as white tee went left.

"Go left, I've got this one," Vanic shouted over his shoulder to the two officers in his wake as he burst through the doors ahead of him. A long corridor of buzzing ceiling lights lit up the fleeing fugitive as he took a left turn up ahead. Vanic gave chase, careful to expect an ambush as he turned the corner, only to see the man continuing his escape through another door up ahead. Digging deep into any reserves he had, he barrelled down the hall and kicked through the door as he approached. Another long corridor with periodic passages to the left and right greeted him along with the sight of the escapee, and more worryingly what looked to be a fire escape door ahead of him. The gap was too wide to close.

He came to a halt, raised his gun with both hands and took aim. He shouted 'freeze' at the exact second he adjusted his aim, realising that he'd automatically aimed for the back of the targets head. A leg shot was what protocol would dictate for a fleeing target.

Orange sweatshirt took a second to look over his shoulder but made no attempt to slow his escape. The sharp whip crack sound of the pistol went off as the shot found its mark, a spray of inky liquid bursting from his left thigh as the bullet passed through it. The seconds ticked past in slow motion as the man registered the hit before carrying on his attempted escape. He was twenty feet from the exit door now and seemed to be trying to calculate whether to maintain his course or take the right corridor just up ahead, to break line of sight.

The moments pause was all that was required to seal his fate as a second round hit him in the left arm just above the elbow. Deciding he would have to break for cover, he moved right towards the bend only to have his body thrown out from under him as he turned the corner.

After firing the second shot, Vanic lowered his pistol and continued to give chase down the hall in time to see the man turn into the next corridor only to then fly backwards out towards him, the full weight of a dirty blonde, heavily bearded dwarf in uniform following immediately behind. Officer Belbeck used this momentum to slam the man into the wall behind and they fell in a shower of plaster and dust onto the ground.

Vanic didn't slow as he closed the gap and laid a kick across the face of the man now atop of the dwarf and he rolled as the foot connected with his jaw in a sickening crack. Wasting no time, both officers overpowered the umbral and had him cuffed and checked for weapons in seconds.

"Thanks for the assist Bharmund. I'd hate to have been the other team back in your college warball days," said Vanic as he brought the criminal up onto his knees.

"Aye, truth be told there was never much glory in it without scoring the points, but that was always my role. Hit or get hit." He beamed. "Are there any more of the bastards coming our way?"

"Shouldn't be, but there was another one in chase, so I'd better check that out. You can get this one out with the others I take it?"

"You betcha. The others are outside. I just got itchy feet you know!"

VANIC QUICKLY MADE HIS WAY BACK THE WAY HE CAME, blood pulsing in his veins and a slight ache in his leg making itself known from that kick. Heading through the door the others had gone into, he only made it a couple of corridors before reaching them, their prize kneeling cuffed and looking in infinitely better shape than he had left his.

"Didn't doubt you boys for a second." Vanic smirked as he approached, taking stock of their quarry.

The two men looked pleased with themselves, and it seemed they hadn't endured much of a scuffle either.

"Absolutely," said the first. "He froze as soon as we drew on him, sir. Obviously, whatever this is, it wasn't worth taking a bullet for."

"Same can't be said for his friend. Looks like he took your share too pal."

The officers gave each other a brief, knowing look.

"He'll be fine. Don't worry. He just wasn't as willing to come peacefully."

What appeared to have been a moment of tension was gone as soon as it arrived, and the officers began to recount the chase in further detail for the detective.

Vanic listened to them describing their pursuit. He knew it helped with morale to let them feel like a win was a win and not just part of the job. His mind was beginning to wander, when out of the corner of his eye he saw movement from their prisoner. Hands still cuffed behind his back he was awkwardly reaching round to his left pocket.

"Wait!" he shouted. But it was too late.

The corridor was filled with a flash of blinding light and an ear-piercing boom, followed by a clatter of metal on concrete.

"Nobody fire. That's an order," Vanic shouted as he rubbed at his eyes, trying to clear his vision. The ringing in his ears left him disorientated as if underwater.

By the time his vision had cleared a few seconds later, he was met with what he feared, two officers looking similarly stunned and an empty pair of handcuffs resting on the man's clothes on the ground. Vanic wasted no time and ran down the corridor after the fleeing man. The halls took three more turns before coming to a door that sadly echoed the fire escape from earlier in the evening.

Vanic ran out the door into the night, making it five yards before something hard hit him from behind. He staggered forward a few steps, trying to maintain his balance, before spinning to find himself face to face with the fleeing man, now naked, his black form practically blending into the surrounding darkness.

The man had a look of absolute hatred plastered across his face and Vanic found himself frozen in place as he began to step towards him.

Every cell in his body was screaming at him to reach for his pistol, but his mind failed him and all he could see was his son's face, broken and fatherless.

The man halted, turning his head as the sound of fast approaching footsteps carried from inside the building. Turning back to focus on Vanic, he leaned in with a sneer. "You'll live to regret this, cop."

An elbow caught Vanic across the jaw and sent him spinning to the ground as the man ran into the night as the officers came rushing from the doorway.

Picking himself up, Vanic bent to catch his breath as the rain washed over him.

"So, you didn't think to search him for weapons, no?" Vanic said as both officers hung their heads like naughty children about to be scolded.

CHAPTER FIVE

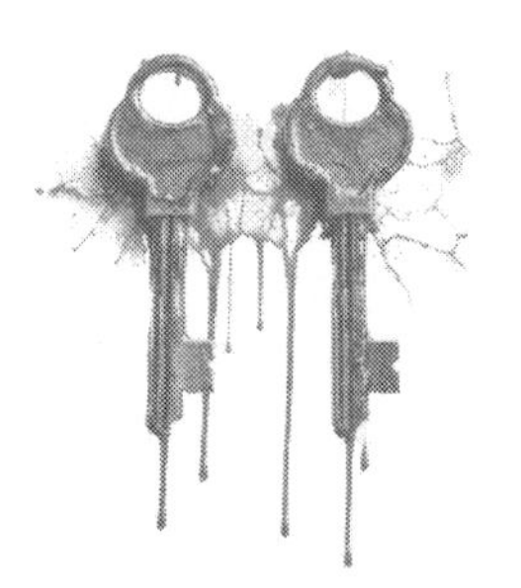

Vanic stood outside the Station with Clara and savoured the last of his cigarette before instantly lighting another. He wasn't what he would currently class as a smoker, but in times of stress or in this case anger and frustration they were a necessity to functioning properly.

"Look, you took down a pretty big street operation, got a bunch of workers and presumably someone higher up in custody, so what if one guy got away? I'd say tonight was a big success for you." Clara was, as always, the eternal optimist.

He exhaled smoke through his nose. "Yeah sure, but it would have been a clean sweep if just for a standard protocol pat down. Day one of training stuff, you know?

That, and I froze. The guy was right there in my grasp and all I could think was – you're about to die."

His mind flashed back to City Hall, and the near-death experience that he'd found plaguing his dreams.

"Well, you can't really change that now can you, so you can either stand here in the cold and smoke yourself to death or you can give yourself a pat on the back and come inside. Your frozen butt is really no concern of mine."

He seethed for a second, letting the rage inside him fester and bubble, needing a release before he looked at his half-finished cigarette and stubbed it out in his left palm with a twisting motion.

Clara winced. "Doesn't that hurt?"

"Like nobody's' business," he said looking her in the eye.

"Then why do it?"

"That's nobody's business." He smirked.

Clara rolled her eyes dramatically at him as she turned to walk back into the station. "Boys." She tutted.

Back inside the station a hum of energy, a buzz of excitement, lingered in the air. In stark contrast to the usual end of Vanic's shifts, the sun slowly made its presence known in the sky and the occupants of the station were quieter. Usually they were fuelled with alcohol having engaged in bar fights, or drunk driving. Women in tiny dresses often had shoes in hand, screaming about something or other that had waylaid their evening. But tonight, while these same people were still in attendance, it felt subdued somehow.

Vanic worked his way through the reception area, past an aforementioned drunk girl with shoes in hand, this one bearing a pink sash proclaiming it was her hen night, as she screamed emphatically in the face of a female officer with a notepad in hand. *What a lucky future husband.* After a brief conciliatory nod to the officer in question, Vanic stepped through the doors into the back of the station.

He continued making his way through the corridors, towards the Forensics and morgue, still seething in his head about what he considered to be a failure on his part this evening. He stepped through a set of black double doors and was greeted by a tall handsome man with short wavy hair that flowed like spun gold in color and texture, his pointed ears poking out through the golden locks. His white shirt sleeves were rolled up to the elbow and he wore a black leather apron that wouldn't look out of place in an abattoir.

"Ahh, the conqueror returns. Why so glum, chum?" His arms were bent, fingers to the sky as if he'd just scrubbed up for surgery.

Vanic had little time for Cylanorr. The elf was always too upbeat for someone who spent a lot of time elbow deep in bodies and while he was a pleasant enough guy, Vanic just found him too much at times.

"A fish wriggling off the hook will do that, Cyl."

"Yes, so I've heard, but you took down a big operation I'm told. Even brought in an umbral with a pulse. Is our lamplighter starting to soften up on us?" He cocked an angular golden eyebrow in Vanic's direction.

Vanic's eyes narrowed. "Don't call me that. It's bad enough the lowlifes of this city giving out names to officers without it being thrown around here too."

Cylanorr smiled in response. "It's just you with a title as far as I'm aware unless I'm just behind with the times. Not much for conversation are my guests generally."

Vanic just stared straight through him.

"Oh, and while we're on that subject. This one." He gestured to the body on the table in front of him. "No surprises. Cause of death: massive head trauma and a broken neck. You'll be pleased to know he'll have basically died on impact. No suffering."

"Well, at least it was the one I caught that was responsible. We can add that to his list of charges. Anything else?"

"No, nothing important. He was covered in residue from the site, so presumably one of the workers."

"Ok, well I guess that's about as much as I was expecting, really. Thanks, Cyl."

With that he headed back out to drop by his desk before hitting his locker and heading home.

THE ROADS WERE QUIET ON THE DRIVE HOME, AS THEY always were at this hour. The sun crested the skyline, casting long shadows from trees and buildings, and small signs of the city came to life, making themselves known. Early morning workers set off for their day, joggers and dog walkers milled about and the remnants of the heavy party goers staggered home like zombies.

For the entirety of the drive back, Vanic replayed the night in his head over and over. The whole operation, the shots he'd fired into the fleeing suspect, and that final kick to the jaw gave him a certain amount of pleasure before he remembered that blinding flash and the other man getting away. His blood boiled as he pulled into his driveway.

He let himself in the front door and slipped off his shoes, before tiptoeing across the hall. The silence and emptiness of the house in daylight always felt strange to him. It was like arriving home from a holiday knowing it hadn't been lived in, even though it had only been hours and Roma would be asleep upstairs.

With as much stealth as he could muster, he tiptoed down the hall into the kitchen and cracked open the refrigerator door, allowing the small arc of light from within to illuminate the room while he found a glass. He filled it with milk from the door shelf and drank in front of the sink before rinsing the glass and heading back out into the hall, closing the refrigerator door with his hip as he went. He made his way upstairs like a silent assassin and brushed his teeth in the bathroom before heading into the bedroom.

He stripped out of his uniform and threw the clothes onto the superfluous chair in the corner of the room, *why anyone would choose to sit in a tiny chair in a room with a perfectly good bed to lay on was a mystery to him*, before climbing quietly into the bed beside the sleeping form of Roma. She stirred briefly before rolling over to nestle into his chest.

Staring blankly up at the ceiling he focused on his breathing, struggling to get the image of the second criminal out of his head.

"Bad day?"

He turned to see Roma staring up at him, her green eyes shimmering with moisture as she blinked rapidly, clearing her sleepy vision.

"Some good, some bad," he said with a dour voice.

"All I'm hearing is, your night didn't exactly finish with a happy ending." She moved up his body. "Let's see what we can do about that."

She pressed her lips hard against his as she brought her leg up across his body, her thigh resting across his crotch.

Vanic was about to protest, when he felt her warm tongue on his and he returned the passion of the kiss, his fingers running through her hair and pulling her into him as he savoured the softness of her lips.

The effect was instantaneous. Blood rushed to his crotch, leaving him standing to attention and banishing the melancholy of the evening as he rolled her onto her back and leaned down to nuzzle into her neck as his hand wandered down to caress the goose-bumped flesh of her breasts. Her nipples were hard with excitement.

She let out a soft moan as his hand continued lower and found the warmth between her legs, bucking her hips and pushing back against his fingers as she again pressed her lips to his.

Pulling away from his embrace, she pushed him back onto the bed and straddled his body before reaching down and guiding him easily inside her, before rhythmically gyrating her hips on top of him.

Vanic gazed up as she passionately rode him, her long hair cascading down over her shoulders and tickling his face. He ran his hands along the curves of her hips and up her body before gripping her and flipping her back onto the bed. He gently entered her again as he fell forward, burying his face into her shoulder as he slowly thrust inside her.

After the initial passion of the moment had passed, the grinning face of the escaped umbral man was now burned back into his mind, taunting him with a twisted midnight leer.

He reached down and cupped his hands under Roma's ass, shifting her axis as he began to pump his hips harder and harder as he slapped against her, a simmering rage now spurring him on.

Moaning in tandem, he soon came to climax and collapsed upon her, their sweating bodies sticking together. He rolled off her and leaned in to kiss her gently on the forehead, the slight salt taste of her perspiration lingering on his lips, before whispering a quiet "thank you," and resuming his position staring at the ceiling until sleep eventually came for him.

CHAPTER SIX

"And you know they're just like you and me." Vanic's father said as he looked down at him.

Vanic looked up into his father's eyes and felt conflicting emotions as he pondered this. The unknown was a scary thing inside his eleven-year-old mind, but he had absolute trust in his father and knew he wouldn't put him in harm's way.

"Yes, I know they look different," his father continued. "But really they are just little boys and girls like you, excited and nervous to be at school."

Vanic was just six when his mother had died, an unavoidable accident involving a bus she was riding and a delivery truck, throwing his barely started life into upheaval. Vanic's father had done an impeccable job as a sole parent from that point forward, but now at eleven, this new change in school life was again set to rock the balance of his world.

A dramatic statement, but a fair one. The continued attempts at proper inclusion of the umbral community had reached the schools, and Vanic was in the age bracket to be part of the first trial. A six-building complex housed under a huge domed ceiling. Bubble school as his father liked to call it. It had its own underground shuttle connecting directly to Fallowport.

After taking a deep breath and blowing it out hard, Vanic puffed out his cheeks like a trumpet player and set off towards the main entrance of the school. He took a quick glace over his shoulder to see his father standing there watching, a thumb in the air and a smile on his face, before hitching up his backpack and setting off up the steps.

VANIC TOOK A SEAT AT HIS DESK AND GLANCED AROUND. Rows of desks, whiteboard, large desk for the teacher, a globe, a skeleton, a wall of clothes hooks and pigeonholes and a small stationary cabinet on wheels. *Ok*, he thought, it does look like a regular classroom. The churning in his stomach began to settle as he familiarised himself with the surroundings.

This lasted all of three minutes. Other children began to spill into what was an otherwise empty classroom and he quickly found himself boxed in with about thirty other students. Taking a quick headcount, he noted nine of the obsidian hued pupils, three girls and six boys. *Not an even split then,* he thought. For some reason this two to one split also seemed to calm him.

From his vantage point in the centre of the back of the class, he surveyed the room again and came to a stop as his eyes met with the girl sat to his left. She sported a mint-green sweater, a slate-grey skirt and polished, red, buckled shoes. Caramel blonde hair was tucked behind both ears, and it framed her face as she gave him a smile, revealing a full set of braces. Feeling his cheeks begin to flush, Vanic returned the smile and decided it best not to linger as he continued to look around. As he turned, he was immediately greeted with the hard stare of the umbral boy to his right. The boy's gaze bore into him, and Vanic wondered if he'd been staring at the back of his head this whole time waiting for him to turn around. The boy wore a powder blue hoodie, grey sweatpants, and black military boots. His stare, Vanic now realised, was more of a scowl.

VANIC WOKE UP WITH A GASP AND TOOK A BREATH. ROMA lay unbothered to his right and the only light in the room was the dim green glow from the alarm next to the bed and the ever-present pinprick red beam from the TV's standby light. A shiver ran down his spine, causing a momentary twitch of his neck before he settled back into his pillow and tried to get back to sleep.

CHAPTER SEVEN

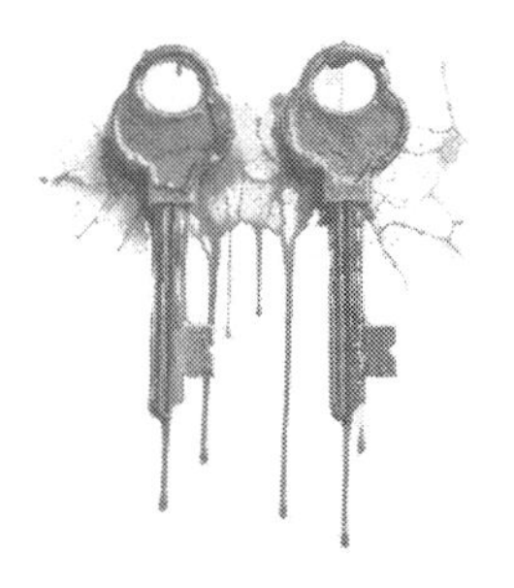

Calvin had a rare morning off work and so decided to head into the Everdawn shopping arcade to find something to wear for the upcoming wedding of his work colleagues Ben and Yasmin. While it was true, he'd only received an invite to the evening celebration and not the ceremony itself, he still felt that it warranted a new suit, nonetheless. In all honesty, he didn't really need much of an excuse to treat himself to a new outfit and the knowledge that a handful of single ladies from the office would be in attendance greatly helped.

Having thankfully missed the crowd of morning commuters clogging up the passageway into the mall, he quickly navigated through the lengthy tunnel entrance and past the food court before taking the escalator up to the second floor towards his destination. The artificial white lights overhead seemed to emit a light thrumming sound once you reached this level, which he found oddly soothing and the general congestion of the walkways up here was always minimal, a bonus for a man on a mission.

Though two decades of minimal maintenance has taken the shine off the complex, it still served as a great milestone in the ongoing attempts to allow proper cohabitation between the sun averse umbral populace and the city of Dalton.

He stood at the top of the escalator and glanced back down at the shoppers and commuters making their way through the mall and thought about how much of the complex was hidden away. The central walkway was sandwiched either side by two levels of storefronts that ran straight and canyon-esque through the domed building and it didn't take a genius to realise than in a circular building that meant a lot of space hidden away to the sides, housing what he assumed to be offices and storage.

As he now glanced around the upper level, pondering where to begin his shopping trip, he heard the crash of a large crate fall. Turning in the direction of the noise he saw a muscular umbral man in navy blue overalls and neon high-vis jacket fighting with a wooden crate of about six or seven feet that had half slipped off the red trolley underneath.

"Apologies if I scared you there. This sucker sort of got away from me, I swear it's the wheels," came the gravelly voice of the man still straining to right his cargo. "Don't suppose you can lend a fella a hand?"

Calvin was not a man to go out of his way to help a person in need, but this interaction had pulled him into the problem in a way that would be more of an issue to dismiss.

"I suppose I can't make it worse," he said as he walked to the edge of the trolley that was sticking out from one of the many corridors that led away from the stores, *The secret areas,* he thought.

"Absolutely not," said the workman as he stepped back to the end of the box still balanced on the trolley. "I think it might be easier if I unload some of the contents and then put it back once we've got it right. Hang on."

With what seemed like minimal effort, the man threw open the top of the box as it let out a creak from the hinges on the other side. Calvin barely had time to register the sparse amount of straw that lined the box as a black blur came at him and a burst of pain erupted in his face. Before he knew what was happening, he was caught by a man he couldn't see and flipped into the crate. Then the lid closed, and darkness enveloped him in both senses of the word.

CHAPTER EIGHT

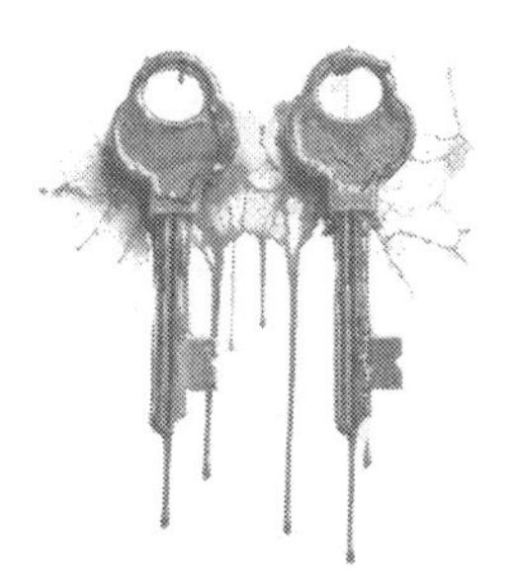

The pink meat hissed as it hit the grill, the juices sizzling and sending up steam.

Vanic rotated the sausages, their skin taking on a dark brown glossy appearance, and he deftly moved them to the side of the barbeque with tongs to allow more space for fresh burger patties. He was not by any stretch of the imagination a '*BBQ master*' and knew his skills were suited to flipping meats and burgers that required very little care. He dreamed of cooking a brisket, carefully seasoning it before leaving it for hours to smoke, finishing up with a tender and juicy end product, like the burly men on the internet created, but he didn't have the time to follow through on it.

The daylight was beginning to dwindle, and the sky took on shades of red and orange, blended beautifully like the most perfectly crafted tequila sunrise. It remained a warm evening and the distant sounds of lawnmowers fighting to beat the sun could still be heard around the neighbourhood. Vanic lifted his beer to his lips and drained the last remnants from the bottle.

"We're gonna need to do a beer run I think." He placed the bottle down, knowing it wouldn't be his job to drive.

At this, Josh turned from his conversation with Roma and her friend Paul and caught Vanic's eye.

"Well, I suppose that means I'm in the saddle then." He placed a hand on the shoulder of each of his companions and politely excused himself. "Just make sure you've got your wallet yeah?"

After doing the rounds of the guests in the garden and a quick provisions check in the kitchen, Vanic and Josh set off in Josh's car heading towards the gas station convenience store that was a twenty-minute drive away. The sun had fully ebbed, and the evening was setting in for the night. The streetlights glowed a warm pink as they came to life.

After navigating minimal traffic on the roads, they arrived at their destination, parked up outside and headed into the store, the tell-tale *squawk* of the door sensor announcing them as they entered.

The fluorescent overhead lighting and bright white everything (floor, counters, shelving) gave the store a sterile aseptic feel. The counter to the left was manned by a heavyset man in his forties and his twentysomething female colleague. Though barely over six feet in height, each of the six shelving units across the three aisles were adorned with a sliding ladder the exact style you would expect to see in a grandiose old library. These served as mild inconvenience to most, but an absolute must for the dwarven community.

Leaving Josh in the aisle to grab snacks, Vanic headed to the back of the store to pick up beer. After taking a moment to let the wall of sodas and insanely coloured energy drink cans mystify him, *some of these cans looked practically futuristic*, he settled on a twenty-four-bottle case with a practical carry handle built into the crate and headed back down the aisle.

He heard the raised voices barely a second before Josh reached out and placed his hand on his chest, barring his way.

"This is a fucking joke, right?" An obsidian figure stood facing the counter, decked out in a black hoodie, dark grey sweatpants, and a pair of black sneakers with garish neon-green plastic detailing running down the sides.

Vanic made a fist with his left hand almost instinctively.

The man behind the counter blinked and Vanic could see that he was beginning to get flustered.

"N...no. No," the man stammered. "We always need to see ID when selling alcohol to anyone." His cheeks reddened.

"Yes, and I just showed you my ID." Aggravation seeped from the man's voice.

"Well yes of course, it's just that you all—"

"We all...," The tone was clear. "We all what?" he spat.

"I... I mean, it's just...well..."

"Go on. Say it," he pushed. "Say we all look alike. Do it."

At this point, Vanic swapped the crate to his other hand and moved to step forward, as he felt Josh's arm hold him back with more force.

"Is there a problem here?" Josh said as he stepped forward instead.

The man turned as he and the counter clerk acknowledged the new arrival to the situation.

"Just a little everyday prejudice, nothing that need concern you," came the response, coiled in tension.

"Well, I don't know about that. I'm... off duty right now, but I am an officer of the law. What is..." he paused for the briefest of moments here. "The issue?"

He could see the clerk's shoulders relax as the obvious shift in body language took over.

"It's just that I need ID for the sale."

Josh reached out to take the ID from the man and as an afterthought added "Can I see that?" A statement more than a question, as he took the card.

He looked it over properly before passing it back. *Twenty-four.* Young, but old enough and quite clearly the man in the photograph.

"This looks all in order to me. I suggest you serve this young man and let him get back to his evening."

"Yeah, and what if I don't want to do my business here anymore?" The young man's back was clearly up from this confrontation.

Vanic found himself momentarily lost in panic as visions of the escaped umbral man filled his mind, and his parting words, *you'll live to regret this*, played on a loop, before he snapped out of it and stepped forward, placing a palm on the man's chest and watching him visibly flinch at the touch. "I suggest... that there is always a place to pick your battles sir. And this isn't one of them."

Vanic watched as the man shrunk away from his grown-up bravado. His shoulders hunched, and he stepped forward to complete the transaction with a teenage sulk before leaving.

Their own purchases were then made with haste. The crate of beer and mountain of chips and snacks that Josh deemed *'commission'*, were bagged up before they headed back out to the car and Josh wasted no time getting into it.

"I had that covered. Why must you always do that?"

Vanic sighed exaggeratedly. "By covered, you mean impersonating an officer? Long answer or short answer?"

"Short answer." He tore into a bag of chips.

"Because I'm a cop and it's the right thing to do."

"Pppphhhhffftttt." He blew his tongue at him. "Nah. Long answer."

"Ok. Because there's a power imbalance and that is always a dangerous thing when it comes to confrontation."

"Right, well I'm gonna need more than that. Explain it to me like I'm five."

"So just like usual then." He smirked. "Ok. Well, here we are in this modern civilised society. We have laws and rules, things that keep me in a job, things that most people abide by. Yeah?"

"I'm with you so far," *h*e said through a mouthful of ridged paprika chips. "Break the law. Get a spanking. Yeah?"

"Exactly. Except that at our core, we're animals." He pondered on this for a second before figuring out how to continue. "So, the big guy, he knows he's a big guy, right? Let's put him in a situation where things could get violent. Now he knows that if things get physical, then he's at risk of getting in trouble. The problem is, he also knows that he always has that as an option. An ironically named 'get out of jail card' if you will."

"Corner an animal and It will fight back?" Josh Interjected.

"That. Exactly. And my point is, when an umbral is concerned, they're always the big guy."

CHAPTER NINE

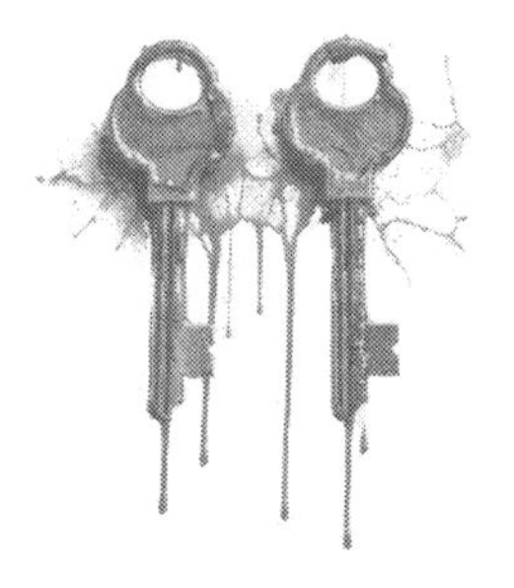

Vanic stared at his reflection in the mirror. The steam from the shower was still blurring the areas he hadn't wiped clean to shave. He felt good.

The last few weeks had been hard going and he'd felt the weight of it all baring down on him and surrounding him in a grey fog of unease. He was actively aware that this caused his mood to be low and left him like a coiled spring, ready to burst at the slightest thing.

He didn't like to dwell on it, but he'd definitely had doubts about his continued career path. With recent events coming far too close to deadly, he was forced to admit that the idea of something fatal happening and leaving his Son without a father, was a new burden he'd been lumped with.

He was not an aggressive man and his temper, even when taken out on others, wasn't violent or threatening but he could easily snap at people if he didn't rein it in.

Today though, he felt at peace. The upset of the' failed' raid was a thing of the past. He'd had time to reflect on it as well as downtime with Roma and friends at yesterday's barbeque and today he would have a day with his son. Noah loved the zoo, and he was sure the addition of the new Vilgore display and performance would have him in joyous fits of childlike wonder.

He towelled his face to remove any remnants of shaving foam, *remembering to get behind his ears*, and scooped a small amount of wax from a small blue tin and worked it into his hands before running it through his hair. After moving through to the bedroom, he quickly threw on some underwear and a pair of black jeans before selecting a navy polo shirt and pulling that over his head, being careful not to flatten his hair.

He would leave the car at Sarah's and take the train in with Noah, avoiding dealing with city traffic alongside a fussy five-year-old.

Vanic was barely a few steps out the door when he stopped dead in his tracks. Something was wrong. That overpowering sixth sense that something was amiss overtook him. *What was it?*

After a few moments he let himself back into the house and grabbed the zoo and show tickets off the counter, their purple metallic shimmer mocking his near disaster.

IT WAS EARLY AFTERNOON BEFORE HE TURNED THE CAR ONTO Sarah's Street. The sun beamed down from a cloudless blue sky, and it was shaping up to be a warm day.

Sarah's home, *formerly their family home*, was set midway up the most classically picturesque street. Rows of trees lined the sidewalks, long lawns led up to clean white houses, and children dashed back and forth through sprinkler systems shouting in glee. The car window was rolled down, and barbequed meat smells carried through the air. Somewhere in the distance a lawnmower could be heard, its high drone a backdrop to the scene. Suburban living at its best.

Vanic pulled into the driveway and could see the front door opening as he stepped out the car. A tall, athletic woman, with sandy blonde hair tied up in a bun wearing blue/purple combination yoga pants and an oversized, much washed and faded classic cartoon t-shirt, *Bucky O'Hare to be precise*, stepped out onto the wooden porch to greet him.

Sarah wore little make-up, *not that she needed it*, and he thought for a second about how grateful he was for their situation. As divorced co-parents, they were on excellent terms with each other, and Sarah felt no need to make any false efforts to look or act a certain way. This wasn't to say she was a slob, far from it, you just got her how she was, no airs and graces.

"Right on time." She met him with a cocked smile. "I've made sure to pour a few bags of skittles down his throat and wash it down with a couple of cokes. You're in for a treat." She raised her eyebrows and bared her gritted teeth in a mock panic gesture before switching back to a smirk.

"And here I thought Dad was supposed to be the poor role model for the kids." He leaned in and gave her a firm squeeze.

"Come on in." She gestured into the open doorway and Vanic got three steps before the stampede of tiny footsteps upstairs made itself known and the whirlwind that was Noah came barrelling down the stairs.

"Dad!" He beamed as he flew into Vanic's outstretched arms.

Vanic lifted Noah up as his little arms wrapped around his neck to hang on tight. He spent a moment just breathing him in, that soap fresh smell was still working in tandem with what Vanic could only describe as innocence. The subtle scent that felt like love and warmth. Family. The smell that made him know that everything was right in the world. No matter how bad things got, he had helped bring this tiny human into the world and that, above everything else, would always be his crowning achievement. At what point did a person lose that smell?

"Dad, Dad, are you excited for the zoo? Will there be lots of animals there?"

Vanic was starting to wonder if there was any truth to him being pumped full of sugar.

"Well, if there isn't I'm going to be having some strong words with whoever runs this empty zoo." He lowered Noah back to the ground. "Are you excited to see the Vilgore?"

"I'm excited to see all the animals!"

"Ok, well that's me told."

He turned his attention back to Sarah as Noah sat his butt on the bottom step of the stairs and began pulling on a pair of tiny white socks.

"You're sure you don't want to tag along?" Vanic asked sincerely.

"Totally." She confirmed with a nod. "I appreciate the offer, but it'll be nice for him to have a day with his dad; and I'll be sure to make use of a day off."

Noah had finished with the socks and was fastening the Velcro straps on his red and white sneakers. He stood up and did a little two-step to check they were comfortable and darted for the open front door. "I'm ready! Let's gooo!"

Vanic took a long breath. He loved that kid, but he was fully aware how much of a handful he was going to be today. He cherished every moment he got to spend with his son, but he was still allowed a moment to prepare for the onslaught.

"Wait a minute, buddy, aren't you forgetting something?"

Noah froze as if struck down by lightning, a brief second of horror covering his face, before he ran back in and planted a massive wet kiss on his mother's lips.

"Sorry Mom. Love you lots. See you later." And he was back out the door.

Vanic echoed Noah's actions and gave Sarah a kiss on the cheek. "I'll try have him back in one piece," he said as he headed out the door behind the four-foot ball of energy that was his son.

VANIC HANDED OVER TWO METALLIC TICKETS AT THE MAIN desk at the zoo' entrance, and in return received two wristbands, embossed with the zoo logo's purple and gold colour scheme and a large fold out map. This was handed to Noah once Vanic had fastened both their wristbands; and they'd carried on through into the zoo.

Upon passing through the main entrance to the park they found themselves in a large circular plaza. Picnic benches were sporadically placed in the centre with gift-shops, cafes and food vendors circling like wagons in a defensive structure around the outside. The smell of pop-corn and hotdogs permeated the very air around them and the background chatter of children and adults alike was the soundtrack to their arrival.

Vanic watched as Noah's face lit up with childlike wonderment and his hazel eyes seemed to practically double in size.

"What do you say we get you some popcorn now and go see some animals before we get some actual food, buddy?"

Noah was fixed on his surroundings, his little eyes darting about the place, and he had yet to see any animals.

"Ok!" his little voice acted on autopilot.

That was about as many syllables as Vanic expected to get from him right now, so placing his hand on his shoulder he began to lead him to the nearest snack vendor.

THE LION STOOD ON THE CREST OF THE HILL, ITS LEFT PAW resting upon a large jutting-out grey slab of stone, its musculature defined across its huge front leg. Its whole form was taut, solid, and obvious even from a distance. What seemed like an oversized feline yawn, slowly turned into a low relaxed roar, the sound deep and hollow as if passed through the empty body of a tree. The resonating call carried across the enclosure effortlessly.

Vanic was frozen in his own moment of wonderment as he gazed on at the lion on the hill, with Noah by his side. The walkways of the zoo seemed to be hewn into the very stone that surrounded them, various open corridors of rock providing directions to follow to the next grass or dirt filled enclosure. They intermittently opened into wider areas for multiple exhibits or space for benches, providing brief respite from the sun and tactically placed ice-cream vendors.

"What about unicorns?"

"What about them?" Vanic knew where it was going, but as a parent, every conversation could be a teachable moment.

"Well, did there used to be unicorns? Like dragons?"

"I don't think so buddy, but maybe."

"But if there used to be dragons and stuff, maybe there used to be unicorns too." There was more than a small amount of hope in his voice.

"You might be right. The reason there isn't any more dragons is because they were too dangerous and would hurt a lot of people." These were the facts, the truth of the matter.

Now was time for the wonder.

"What do you think? Do you think the unicorns were dangerous?" As Van said this, he immediately steepled his hands together in front of his forehead and jutted forward at Noah with a mock growl, poking him in the tummy.

"Daaaad," he whined, then giggled so hard he nearly dropped the last remnants of his hot dog.

"You're probably right. Maybe they're just hiding somewhere."

After spending a couple of hours wandering the zoo, taking in the sights, and the animals, they stopped for ice-cream, drinks, and more hotdogs, though Vanic had decided on a burger. Overpriced and underwhelming as it was.

"Are you feeling about ready for the main attraction?" he asked.

"Vilgores?" His little eyes lit up again and a large, ketchup-stained grin crested his face.

"Exactly that."

CHAPTER TEN

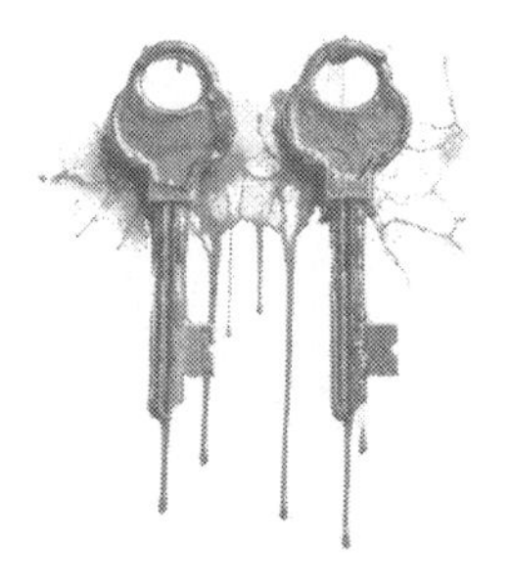

Van and Noah followed the rustic wooden signposts leading the way to the auditorium near the back of the zoo.

A large banner ran across the top of the entrance, drooping in the middle and giving the appearance of an overhanging stomach, gently flapping in the warm breeze. Replete with the trademark golds and purples, the banner announced the impending shock and awe of the Vilgore performance as well as providing swooping winged silhouettes and an unfortunate looking, *though likely well paid*, bucktoothed young boys face of wonder at the forefront.

Holding Noah's hand, Vanic could feel the nervous excitement literally emanating from him like a vibrating wave of childlike joy. He savoured the feel of this small clammy hand gripping tighter as they approached the building. While he certainly had a warm, loving parent growing up, Vanic also had a lot of sour memories from his childhood that further strengthened his need to see Noah happy.

Shaking off his momentary lapse into melancholy, Van led Noah through the doors into an immediate gloom. The inside of the auditorium was noticeably and intentionally much darker inside and the air had a musty, damp quality to it. The smell of popcorn had returned as well as something earthy and almost barnyard-like.

Vanic handed the tickets to the lady in the box office, through a thick layer of glass. Her pleated uniform was black with a blood red trim that ran along the length of the jacket but also provided bold epaulettes. She tore the tickets and passed them back with an emphatic smile, her sharp angular cheekbones and full face of stage make-up doing nothing to diminish the sinister ringmaster look. She pointed them in the direction of another set of doors with another waiting attendant.

The next attendant, *or spawn of evil as Vanic had begun to think of them*, was a tall, gaunt man with a large, hooked nose and hair that though fairly short, was wiry and jutted out from his scalp in gravity defying angles also wore the same black and red uniform; though Vanic could see that the trousers had a single red embroidered stripe that ran the outside of each leg.

He greeted them with another winning smile, *Zygomaticus muscles were certainly earning their keep here*, and took the proffered tickets for inspection.

"Ohhh." His voice had a high nasal quality that carried surprisingly well with the now raised eyebrows.

"Now these are some wonderful seats. Someone is a lucky boy."

Noah seemed entirely oblivious to how creepy everyone in here appeared, his eyes now the size of dinnerplates.

"You're going to have an absolutely fantastic view of the whole performance. Do enjoy, little man." He ruffled Noah's hair as he passed the tickets back.

"Thanks," was all Vanic could muster. *Where did they hire these people?*

The man backed up to push open the large wooden door and gestured in with a long, though delicate arm.

"Oh, and Dad..." A moment of uncomfortable eye contact ensued. "Don't forget to check under the seats." He winked.

As they stepped through the doorway, the whole scene changed. The inside of the auditorium was a complete facsimile of a circus big top. What was from the outside, a huge metallic spire, now rose to the peak of a tent, with ropes and brightly coloured canvas strips lining the ceiling. Spotlights covered multiple areas of the roof and rotated on mechanical devices that bathed the hall in light.

The lower half of the hall was a huge bowl of seats that circled an expansive stadium, the ground a dusty dry earthen surface. Multiple entrances were dotted around the hall, mirroring the one they'd just stepped through, and there was a large set of red doors at the northernmost point that presumably the performers entered from. The auditorium slowly started to fill up as families spilled in.

Vanic led them down to the lowest aisle, where just a circle of fencing separated them from the stadium, and he quickly located their seats. Noah sat to his right, and he took a seat before deciding to reach underneath as the usher had suggested.

The red leather was cool to the touch and as he reached under, he could feel the thick folds of leather bunched up where it had been sewn to the seat. The back of his fingers grazed the bristly texture of the cheap carpeting as he felt about for something. Nothing there.

Maybe this was just part of his act, an odd *'don't look behind you.'* to unsettle the guests. He reflected on the peculiarity of this for a moment and realised the empty seat to his left was technically also his and carelessly reached his left hand under it. His fingers touched something.

After a little manoeuvring, he came up with a small gift box. Eight inches long and about two inches deep, it resembled a jewellery box, though the design was more fitting as a birthday gift. He wasted no time in opening it up and was greeted with a single gift certificate.

"Look buddy," he said as he gently elbowed Noah, who was still taking in the splendour of the room.

"What is it?"

"It's a voucher to get your very own Vilgore teddy from Built-a-Bear. How cool is that?"

Was it some kind of bribe? It all felt a little too much for a freebie.

"Wow that's awesome!" Noah beamed.

"The mall isn't too far away. Do you want to go get it before we head home if there's time?"

The Everdawn Mall, the location of the nearest Build-a-Bear, was only a couple of stops away on the train and Vanic was sure they could get there before it closed.

"Yeah. Can we please?" His voice was polite and full of excitement.

He dithered on the idea for a while as Noah looked up at him with those big, pleading eyes.

It wasn't too far out of their way, but it would be cutting it fine. Maybe it would be better to go back another day, he didn't even need to be there personally and incurring the wrath of Sarah if they were out too late was also a concern.

He quickly realised that at this moment, any alternative planning would mean saying no to Noah, and he wasn't about to put a dampener on their day out.

"We absolutely can."

THE PERFORMANCE LASTED ABOUT FORTY-FIVE MINUTES, which to a child is like literal hours. The lights dimmed and the show began; to fanfare and a variety of entertainers spilling out into the arena doing somersaults and cartwheels. There was fifteen minutes of trapeze acts and various acrobatics before the main event. *Time to be filled*, Vanic thought. There was only so much you could make animals do.

Once the Vilgore were brought out the whole atmosphere in the arena changed. The crowd became hushed except for the occasional *oohs* and *ahhs*.

Three of the strange creatures elegantly strutted out into the arena. With black furred bodies that resembled a panther, they had voluminous manes that circled their large heads. Large, red, insect-like eyes sat under two spindly antennae and a long-coiled proboscis that served as the creature's mouths. Attached to their forelegs and running across their backs were large leathery batlike wings that lay pinned to their sides as they walked.

After some circling of the arena, they began to perform simple tricks: jumping through flaming hoops, performing perfect backflips and other acrobatics before taking to the sky. With an obviously rehearsed coordination the creatures circled the arena from the air, periodically swooping low over the audience, to the great amusement of the crowd.

Vanic felt the air whoosh past him as they flew by, and Noah let out a small high-pitched squeak of joy.

Not long after this, the creatures returned to the handlers at the centre of the arena and the show was transformed into more aerial acts before finishing up with combined tricks with the aerialists up high, catching acrobats mid-air and transferring them to the waiting arms of their partners being the highlight of their talents.

Once the show was over and the beasts and performers had retired for a well-earned break before the next performance, Vanic turned to Noah, who's mouth had been open for the entire performance and with a finger on his chin, popped his mouth closed and began to usher him along the aisle into the rest of the exiting crowd.

They still had plenty of time to get over to the mall and finish off the day with a vilgore teddy for his son.

CHAPTER ELEVEN

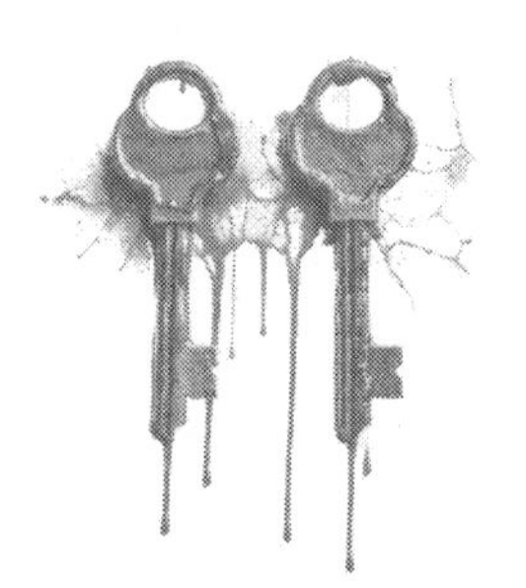

Vanic had quickly and expertly manoeuvred Noah through the crowd and out of the auditorium. Time wasn't completely of the essence, but he didn't want to risk dawdling and miss the mall before it closed. The Everdawn mall wasn't far from home, but it made sense to do it now, rather than making it a whole trip of its own on another day. Plus, he wanted to see another heart-melting smile from Noah, especially after he'd been so good and patient at the show.

Thankfully Bowling Square station had an underground tube line that would take them straight through to the mall, built specifically as a connecting point between Fallowport and the city. A short train journey would get them to the mall before it closed, with enough time to avoid being one of those irritating shoppers that turned up right as a store was getting ready to close.

Vanic held onto Noah's hand tightly as they left the tube station and made their way up the escalators and out into the long cylindrical tunnel that was the entrance to the mall. Looking behind him, he could see the large glass doors that served as the main exit from the mall and through them, he could see that the sun was slowly starting to wane, the coppery hues of early evening setting in.

The long tunnel ceiling was inlaid with rows of circular lights and as they walked away from the exit, the immediate awareness of natural light faded from view making way for an artificial and clinical brightness. The entirely of the inside of this domed mall was affixed with a permanent artificial daylight to accommodate the shadowy umbral community.

There wasn't a great deal of traffic in the tunnel and most of it was heading in the direction of the exit. Families laden with bags shuffling out towards the exit and solo shoppers, or indeed people just passing through making a much swifter attempt at egress.

Vanic was used to crowded areas but was thankful for the lack of people when it came to travelling with Noah. He had this persistent and annoying paranoid fear of him being jostled and herded away into a crowd of people like a child lost in the tide at sea. Which, now he thought about it, was exactly how he felt about Noah near any body of water.

As they reached the end of the tunnel, the mall opened into the sprawling corridor of illuminated store fronts and escalators.

A distant soundtrack of classical music was being pumped out through the speakers, splicing with the background hum of travelling shoppers and commuters.

Just inside the entrance was a large map of the mall displayed on a Perspex billboard, complete with the standard *'you are here'* arrow in a vibrant red.

Stopping for a moment to get their bearings, Vanic studied the map while Noah slowly spun in a circle, eyes to the sky, taking in his surroundings. Build-a-Bear was just over halfway across the mall, past the food court and just before two sets of stairs leading up to the second floor.

Vanic had always considered himself excellent with directions. Something he prided himself on with his work was the attention to minute details. This transferable skill worked well with planning a course, taking note of the expected landmarks to be aware of as well as the general location. They still had plenty of time to make it before closing.

They made it to the store in no time, and general footfall was tapering off as the mall started to wind down ready for closing.

Heading inside there was an overpowering smell of sweet, candy-like perfume and sawdust mingling in the air and the entire inside of the store was painted in glossy reds and sunny yellows with large clockwork cogs and pulleys arrayed around the store ticking away happily.

There appeared to be only two members of staff at present, a young dark-haired girl in a powder blue sweater sat behind the register, blowing her bangs out of her eyes, and an umbral guy in tan chinos and bubble-gum pink sweater which contrasted greatly against his obsidian form. The latter was approaching them at this moment.

"Hello there, folks," he said as he reached them, his broad smile reminding Vanic of the many hosts on kids TV shows he'd endured in recent years.

"What can we get for you today?"

Vanic pulled out the gift box and removed the voucher before presenting it to the man. "We've got this voucher for a vilgore teddy for my son. I assume this is correct?"

The man took the voucher between the finger and thumb of both hands and brought it to eye level, like he was inspecting a piece of rare art, before turning that sickly smile back on.

"Well, isn't that fantastic, what a lucky little man. And what's your name, friend?" he asked as he cocked his head towards Noah like some sinister, sugar-coated bird of prey.

"Noah." Noah's eyes were wide, and he looked wrapped up in the full charade.

"It's nice to meet you Noah, my name's Teorre." He tapped the golden name badge on his chest. "Do you want to come and help me bring your teddy to life?"

"Yes please." Noah replied, the excitement flushing his cheeks.

Vanic stood in the store doing his best to avoid small talk with the assistant as he got to work on Noah's teddy. Realistically, this was Noah's treat, and he didn't need to be a part of it. He was sure the guy was just being polite, but he just wasn't in the mood right now, so he busied himself with intensely inspecting the pile of *'animal skins'* in front of him, rolling the flattened paw of a teddy bears arm between his thumb and forefinger. There was something deeply unsettling about this large mass grave of limp, lifeless teddies that lay before him.

This macabre thought was suddenly dashed from his head when a shrill ear-splitting scream resonated into the store from outside, rising in pitch like the dramatic shriek that might sound from a starlet of old black and white horror movie classics.

Without hesitation, Vanic rushed out of the doorway and into the main thoroughfare of the mall and froze as he surveyed the area.

The source of the wailing was a middle-aged woman in a smart grey pantsuit, who was still screaming as she looked up towards the overhead walkway. A small cluster of people had gathered around her and were also looking towards the upper level, slack jawed expressions painted across their faces.

Vanic looked up and an immediate shockwave ran through him, sounds around him began to feel distant and muffled as his blood ran cold.

Hanging from the side of the walkway, bound, and suspended by rope, was a man with his head lolling to the side, his throat brutally cut, a jagged tear of flesh grinning like a second mouth. Lank hair clung to the grim rictus of his colourless face and there was fresh blood soaking down the front of his body and dripping rhythmically onto the floor below as the body gently swayed.

Around his neck hung from more gore-soaked rope, was a large cardboard sign.

Two words were scrawled grotesquely across it in blood and the obvious roughness of it left Vanic to assume it had been written with a finger.

'Welcome, Detective...'

CHAPTER TWELVE

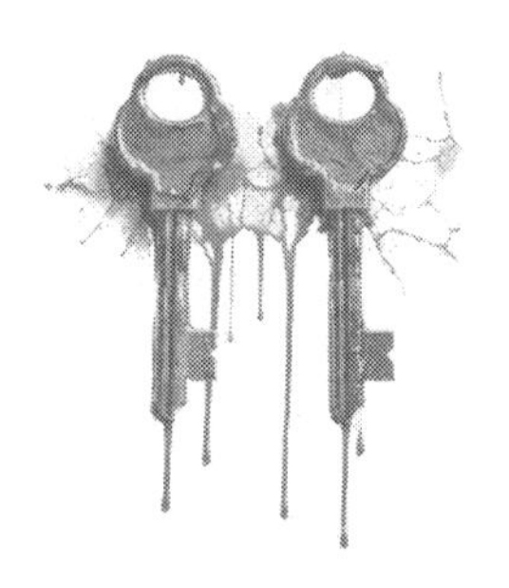

D*rip.*

Drip.

Blood ran down the open throat of the corpse in a slow ebb that flowed across flesh and fabric indiscriminately before reaching the feet where it soaked into the white converse trainers like red wine into carpet. The crimson liquid carried on its course running down the length of the laces that hung loose before dripping like the gradual first rain of the season onto the ground below.

Drip.

The incessant scream of the lady in the pantsuit died down as she was embraced by a small cluster of onlookers seemingly holding it together better than she was.

Drip.

A father covered his young daughters' eyes with his hand as his partner clung desperately to his arm in a vice-like grip, a look of sheer horror branded on both their faces.

Drip.

In stark contrast, a young elven man with hair the colour of burnt sunset stood feet apart, phone in hand filming the whole scene; his face level and calm with a slight incline to one side of his mouth. *Was that a sneer or a smile?*

Drip.

Like breaking the surface of water, the droning hum cut out as sound normalised around him in a sudden snap.

Vanic instinctively reached for the gun at his hip. A gun that wasn't there.

"Fuck."

He wasn't on duty. He wasn't equipped for this. There was little doubt in his mind that this gory display was for him though, the message and the timing were way too convenient to be a coincidence.

Quickly surveying the area, he could see the crowd had grown to twenty-five to thirty onlookers, presumably drawn to the screams. Noah stood in the doorway to the store, the umbral assistant behind him with a hand on each shoulder in what looked to be both a supportive nurturing gesture and a means of stopping the child running into danger.

Vanic's mind raced.

For the body to have only just been noticed, whoever had done this would certainly still be in the mall. He needed to act fast before that small window of time was gone.

The immediate sound of hurried footfall on tile became apparent behind him and Vanic spun and adopted a defensive stance as a slightly overweight, red-faced man came hurtling in his direction.

"Oh shit."

The man came to a halt as he took in the scene. Mirroring Vanic's recent attempt, he unsnapped a pistol from the holster at his side and clumsily drew it.

"Hey. Hey, sir." Vanic waved his arms above his head, gesturing for attention from what he could now see was a member of the mall security.

To his credit, the man didn't raise his gun as he turned and noticed Vanic. He headed over to him with the pistol still facing southward. Vanic could see a small bead of sweat running down the man's temple. This wasn't an everyday occurrence for the poor guy.

Evidently still out of breath, he wheezed slightly as he approached. "What in the hell is going on?"

"I'm sorry," Vanic said as he again gestured with both holds, palms out in front of him in a placating manner.

"I'll explain what I can in a minute, but we don't have a lot of time. I'm a police detective, is there a way to seal the exits immediately?"

"The exits?" he said, with a look that told Vanic that this guy was in well over his paygrade right now.

"Yeah. Yeah, I can seal the doors and put the mall into a lockdown. You said you're a cop?"

"Yes. Now quickly we don't have a lot of time. Just do it. I'll accept full responsibility."

He considered the information and took another glance up at the still hanging body before immediately rushing over to a black metal cabinet affixed to the far wall, unlocking it with a key from the fob on his belt. He swung it open to reveal a metal panel of switches and dials and placed another circular key into a slot in the display and turned it.

There was a brief flicker around them as all the lights in the building went out for half a second and a high single tone rang out across the mall like the chime of a bell.

The flustered guard headed back across to where Vanic was stood. The crowd around them was steadily growing as people gravitated towards the scene of the crime.

"It's done." The security guard said as he returned. "Though you should know, we've also just turned the mall into a complete dead zone, no phone signal or reception gets in or out."

"That's fine, we just need to contain this right now and make sure whoever was responsible can't leave." Vanic realised with dread that his son was also bearing witness to what was going on.

"So." He paused. "I don't suppose it's going to be as simple as you having seen what happened, right?" the guard said with a combined air of both hope and doubt.

Vanic looked again at the hanging body and decided to hold his tongue for the moment. The sign was now coated in more dripping blood but was still legible: '*Welcome Detective.*'

It felt like the most perverse greeting card. Aimed directly at him. Mocking him with its acknowledgement. *Could this be the repercussions of letting that criminal escape?*

"Unfortunately not," he said calmly. "But I was right here moments after it happened, so the killer won't have had time to get away." He was fully in work mode now and his logistical analysis was working overtime.

"They will have fled along the upper level after they threw the body over but even at a full sprint, they won't have had time to make it to an exit before you locked it down. There are just the two exits, correct?"

"There are a couple of loading gates for deliveries, but they will have locked down too and even if they knew the way out the back, it would take longer to reach them than the main exits. I think it's safe to say you've hindered their escape."

Vanic surveyed the crowd again. Now fifty plus onlookers were huddled in smaller groups about the vicinity.

"Ok, well first off we're going to need to get that body down."

"Right, of course," he agreed, a visible grimace on his face.

"Then we're going to need to round up everyone in the building. Get a complete headcount and start asking questions. I think with everyone already gravitating here naturally, this is an unfortunately ideal spot."

"Sounds like you've got this all mapped out at least, officer…?" he finally remembered to ask, looking relieved that someone else was taking control.

"Vanic Bradley. Van is fine," he responded. "And yours?"

The answer came in the form of a shout from across the walkway.

A door to the right of the black security box had opened and a female form burst out. A short obsidian woman in a white button-down shirt, knee length charcoal grey skirt with matching blazer and waxy blood-red heels walked towards them, her long shadowy hair flowing like tendrils of midnight behind her.

"Charles," she piped. "What on earth is going on?"

The umbral woman made a beeline for Vanic and the security guard.

"Just Chuck." The guard murmured.

Vanic watched as Chuck seemed to gain a couple of inches as he stood to attention, sweeping the back of his sleeve across his sweaty brow.

"Miss Melda," he greeted. "As you can see, things aren't too great about now. This is Detective Bradley, he was on the scene from the beginning, and he's been very helpful thus far."

She looked Vanic up and down, a gesture that didn't go unnoticed by him and he felt an instant dislike for this woman building inside him.

"It's you we have to thank for the system lockdown I suppose?" she said in a tone that Vanic couldn't truly register.

"Indeed." He nodded. "It seemed prudent to prevent any exit strategy immediately. You are in charge I assume?" He offered a hand towards her.

Taking the offered handshake, she nodded, and her features seemed to soften slightly.

"I am the acting manager here at Everdawn, yes. I oversee the general day to day running of the facility and its staffing as well as coordinating with each department."

A single yes would have sufficed.

"Yeah ok, that's great. I've already spoken to Charles here about gathering everyone inside to this area for questioning and to get a full head count. I'll need a full list of staff on rota, but can you confirm for me the headcount for security on site please?"

A brief flash of annoyance showed that she wasn't used to being the one taking orders, but that passed quickly.

"Certainly. Well, there is Charles here." She gestured. "And we have two other security members on site. They are stationed in the surveillance room with the CCTV screens. They take alternating shifts to walk the grounds of the mall unless required urgently."

She finished reeling off this information, like a proud pupil that had just expertly spelled out *'monosyllabically'* before she saw the look Vanic was giving her and froze.

"You're telling me there are two members of security sat looking at CCTV of the whole mall right now?" Vanic asked in a cold tone.

"Well…." She was slowly catching his meaning. "Yes?"

"Then why aren't they here right now?"

CHAPTER THIRTEEN

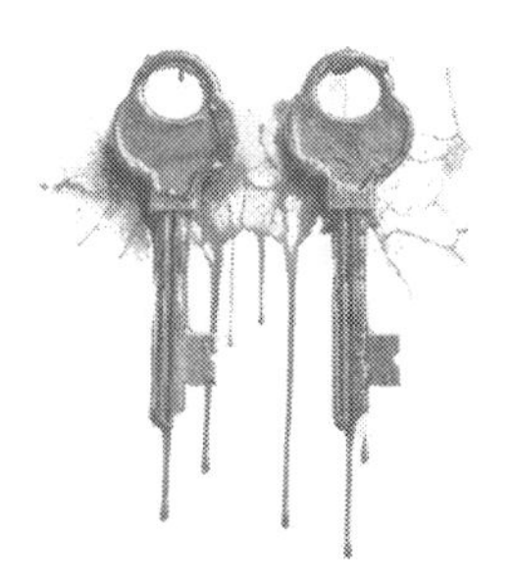

The gentle pairing of piano and strings that had previously served as a musical backdrop in the mall now became an almost mocking melody as the realisation of events started to fall into place.

Taking a moment to make sure Noah was ok and that he would stay alongside Charles and the Build-a-Bear employee who had seemingly formed a protective bond with the child, Vanic was swiftly on the heels of the umbral manager as she headed to a door on the opposite side of the mall from which she'd first appeared.

They stepped through into a long corridor with doors sporadically placed along the left wall. The ceiling rose to a height of about thirty feet and had a series of porthole like windows along it, casting down natural five-foot diameter spotlights onto the ground in the centre of the walkway.

Vanic watched as Melda methodically dodged around these points as she walked.

"Not the most convenient structural aesthetic, I have to admit." She hugged the right wall. "You learn to work round it quite quickly though. Not that it's much of a concern at this point in the day really."

"Yeah, I can see how it would be annoying." He looked up to the ceiling. "They don't open though I assume?"

"Not to my knowledge. Though I think reaching them would be a feat in of itself really."

He took a quick look in the small window of the nearest door as he passed. A row of lockers, a small grey table, and a few plastic chairs. Evidently one of what he assumed to be many staffrooms laid out throughout the building.

They carried on in silence along the corridor as it gradually curved round to the left, eventually coming to a set of stairs leading up before Vanic spoke.

"I think it's better if I take the lead from here." He placed a hand on her shoulder to stop her ascent.

"You'll get no argument from me." She pressed her back to the wall to let him pass. "The security office is just at the top of the stairs anyway."

At the top of the stairs the corridor carried on to their right and Melda pointed to the first door before them, being sure to make no sound.

For a moment he considered knocking on the door and thought better of it. Probably not the smartest idea if there was a killer in waiting.

Taking hold of the cool metal handle, he braced himself and leaned into the solid wooden door as he opened it, the door swinging open upon his weight and suddenly halting halfway as it hit something with a dull thud.

Cautiously stepping into the room, he took in his surroundings - Both side walls of this perfectly square room were lined with olive-green metal filing cabinets, and the far wall was filled with TV screens abuzz with static facing a large kidney-shaped wooden desk with two chairs placed before it.

Slumped back in one of the chairs lay the body of a man, his head lolled backwards facing the ceiling. The obvious pallor of his flesh was the first sign they were too late. The stringy strips of flesh that dangled down from one side of his throat, coated in deepest crimson gore was the other.

On the floor in front of him where the door had stopped, lay the body of a second man, face down in a seeping pool of blood.

Unsure of the state of this second figure, Vanic dropped to a knee and rolled the man over onto his back.

His khaki uniform shirt was shredded in multiple places across his body, the frayed edges of fabric mingling with the pink torn flesh beneath. Four deep gouges also swept across his face, one having practically severed the man's nose, leaving this blood-soaked visage to resemble that of a man pushed face first into a blender.

He moved to futilely check on the second figure before realising Melda had also stepped into the room, a look of abject terror on her face.

It was unsettling to Vanic as he couldn't recall ever seeing a member of the umbral community display such an emotion. Her haunting white eyes were open wide, and her mouth hung open revealing rows of shark-like black teeth.

"They're both gone," he said calmly as he checked over the body in the seat. "I would guess that whoever did this got to this poor guy first before he had a chance to defend himself. The other one looks like he put up a fight."

She stood frozen in place and after making no attempt to respond he continued.

"Both their guns are gone too. That's a concern."

Her head seemed to spasm for a second as if coming out of a trance, followed by a visible full body shiver.

"How….." she paused. "How are you so calm about all of this?"

The question stumped him. He hadn't had a minute to really stop and think, his instincts taking over, and he knew he needed to keep it up, focus on the task at hand and not let his own worries get in the way.

"I was going to ask you the same thing back downstairs. You didn't seem fazed by the poor guy swinging from your walkways. I guess it's just taken a while to catch up to you."

He took something from the waist of the body slumped in the chair and moved back over to the other man and crouched down, before coming back up with two sets of keys.

"Whoever they are, they didn't feel the need to take their keys though. Can you confirm exactly how many sets there are onsite?"

With her faculties apparently back in place she didn't pause. "Four. Myself and the three members of security."

"Ok, well assuming you still have yours, that means he doesn't have any way out of here. Which is potentially a bonus." He pocketed both sets of keys.

"Potentially?"

"Well, the way I see it, this is obviously a planned-out thing. I can't understand why they wouldn't plan for a lockdown. Usually, your escape route is going to be a big part of any crime."

"So, you're saying what exactly?" The evenness of her voice was starting to return.

"That perhaps leaving wasn't their intention."

With this bombshell dropped, he proceeded to check over the room.

To the right of the mounted screens was a large black metallic box with a plethora of cables that fed into it, most of which were shredded or yanked out. That would explain the wall of static they were currently looking at. On the desk was a rather basic looking olive-green telephone, also shredded at the cord. This was starting to seem less and less like a situation Vanic wanted to be part of.

He pointlessly lifted to the phone to his ear anyway and was met with dead silence.

Placing the receiver back down he stepped over to Melda, who was now kneeling at the body of the savaged guard.

"Phone's dead." He placed a hand on her shoulder and flinched at his choice of words.

"I assume there are more static phones in the building?"

She slowly stood up to her full height and gave him a vacant stare before again snapping to her senses.

"Yeah, there are a few phones scattered about. There's one in my office we can use. How bad do you think this is?"

He was mentally on the clock now and knew the best way to field these questions was to be decisive in action and delegate tasks. People panicked less if they were kept busy.

"It's really difficult to say," he said, perhaps too honestly. "We have no idea if this is a lone assailant or not, but what we do know..." He began to count off on his fingers.

"They have killed at least three people."

"They are armed and dangerous."

"They're currently locked inside, with to our knowledge no means of escape."

He looked from Melda to his hand, thumb and two fingers raised like a mock child's replication of a gun, before popping a third finger up.

"And it appears." He paused for a second to figure out if there was a better way to word this. "That they're trying to cut off our communication with the outside."

As it turns out, there was no way to drop that information delicately and the look on her face confirmed it.

"Ok, so that's the bad news," she said. "So where do we go from here?"

"Well first off, we need to get to a phone so I can speak to my chief and get a taskforce down here. After that we need to gather up everyone in one place for their safety and for questioning. Hopefully Chuck has everyone still gathered where we left them."

She nodded at this and waited for him to continue. "Ok, sounds good."

"Where's your office? We should check there first."

"We passed it on the way up, it's at the bottom of the stairs. Do you think it will be safe?"

Vanic pictured Noah's wide-eyed face in a store not too far away and swallowed hard before shaking the thought away. "Only one way to find out. Lead the way."

CHAPTER FOURTEEN

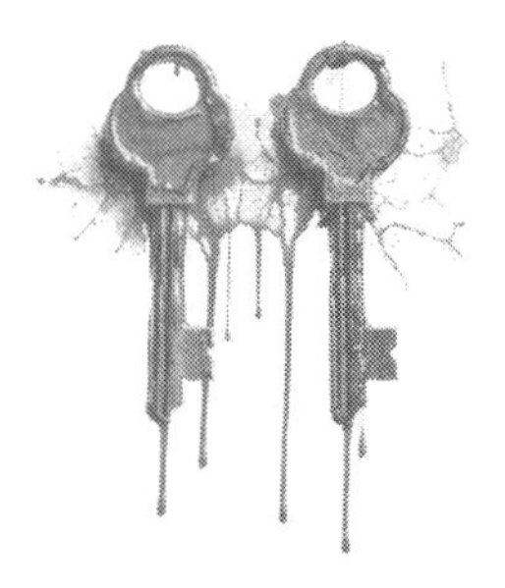

They stepped back out into the hall and Vanic made sure Melda had locked the door before they moved on. It was eerily silent in the corridor and given recent events, he was much more guarded and aware of his surroundings as they descended the stairs.

Back on the lower level they headed to the right of the corridor as she led him to a solid wooden door with a narrow metallic nameplate affixed to it. *Ms M. Verallon, Assistant Manager,* and proceeded to unlock it.

Stepping inside, Vanic was unsurprised to see a rather cold and clinical looking office. A long wooden desk flanked either side by a chair, complete with a computer, another olive-green telephone, and a mail tray. Behind the desk was a grey filing cabinet and the back wall was adorned with a large corkboard covered in what he assumed to be a staff rota. The whole office was devoid of any personality. No plants, photographs or anything that might identify its owner. There wasn't even any sticky notes plastered about the place that you would expect to see in any office space.

This, paired with his so far brief interaction, made him realise that while she was obviously a woman geared towards doing her job to the utmost level, he still didn't think there was any part of her training that would have prepared her for the situation she was currently in.

Moving around the desk, he picked up the receiver and listened in relief to the heavenly sound of a dial tone.

"Why don't you head back out to the others, and I'll be right there once I've made the call?" he said gently. "If you can help get people gathered as much as possible that would be great. Also, if you could discretely let Chuck know that whoever is out there is armed, that would be ideal."

She nodded and placed her keys down on the desk before heading out into the corridor.

He hated to think it, but she was probably more than up to the task of keeping the crowd out there in line.

Once she was gone, he dialled the direct number for the chief, who picked up on the fourth ring. Quickly and methodically, like reading off a report, he filled him in on all the details he had. Body count, sabotage of CCTV and the phone, and a rough idea of civilians present, though that was an absolute guess at this point.

The chief let him finish his report before confirming he would be on his way immediately with as many men as he could gather and to continue keeping everyone together in one place while he waited. 'No heroics,' he said gruffly.

Vanic placed the receiver back down and considered that for a second. He had absolutely no desire to be heroic today, especially not with Noah out there too.

He began to head for the door when that thought came back around again.

Sarah.

He should really call her too and let her know what's going on. She would likely be expecting them back about now.

Taking a deep breath in through his nose and slowly letting it loose past his lips, he sat back at the desk and made the call.

"What's wrong?" she said as soon as she heard his voice.

"You know, we usually start a call with hello." He tried to squeeze hold of a level of normality.

"Sure, but what's wrong? Is Noah ok"' He could hear the panic in her voice.

"Yeah, he's fine. Absolutely fine. But we have run into a problem."

"What sort of a problem?"

"We were at the mall, you know, Everdawn? We were getting him a Build-a-Bear. There's been a homicide."

Silence on the other end of the line.

"Well actually, there's been three, that we know of. Anyway, the malls been put into a lockdown. I've called the chief already and he's on his way, but I don't know how long that's going to be."

"But Noah is fine? You're sure?"

"I promise you. He's fine. It looks like I'm gonna be here a while, but as soon as the chief gets here, I'll have one of the guys drive Noah back to you."

More silence. And then "Ok, well you don't let him out of your sight until then, you got it? Don't make me come down there."

He let out a small chuckle.

"Sarah, I think I was meant to be here. Like it's for my benefit."

"What do you mean?" She sounded worried again.

"It happened right by us, and there was a sign on the body. Welcome detective."

Even more silence, though he could hear her breathing had accelerated.

"I think the killer is umbral. In fact, I've got pretty strong suspicions on who. I let someone get away recently, and I'm worried that they're seeking revenge."

"Listen, you get back to our son and you wait for the cavalry to show up. You hear me? Van, no heroics."

"That's what the chief said. I'll speak to you soon."

"Stay safe."

He heard the click at the line went dead.

He thought about calling Roma too, but they'd spoken in the past about her desire to know as little as possible about his work life. While she was proud of him, she didn't like the idea that he was out every night putting himself in harm's way. They would probably be out of here soon anyway.

CHAPTER FIFTEEN

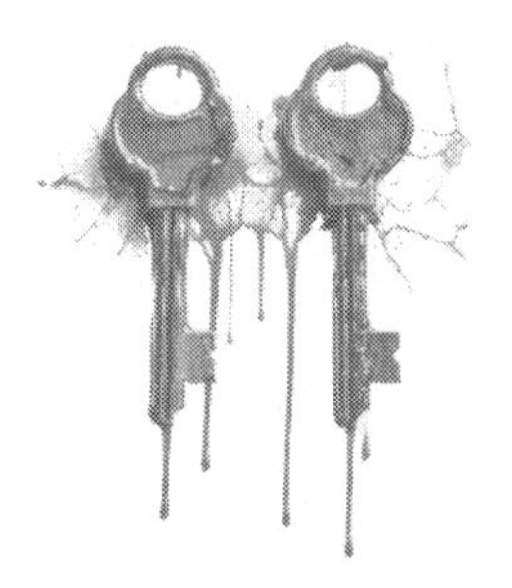

When Vanic stepped back out into the storefront area of the mall, he was greeted with a scene of chaos.

There were over a hundred people gathered in the area now. All huddled in groups and making their presence known in small outbursts.

Chuck and Melda were dealing with a large group of irate women, fronted by an overweight red-faced woman with bottle-blonde curls and an entire outfit of Lycra. Even from a distance, the spittle flying from her lips could be seen violently exiting her mouth.

Three other clusters of school-run mom groups scattered about as well as smaller gatherings of people, who seemed to be taking the gravity of the situation a little more seriously.

The screaming woman was sat on a smooth metallic bench alongside the family with the young daughter and two other men. Their attempts to calm her seemed to have worked and though still sobbing this was just background noise in the general buzz of the crowd.

Over at Build-a-Bear Noah was still standing with his midnight protector, though their group had also grown to about a dozen. A cursory glance would confirm that each of their number was dressed in some manner of uniform and so was fair to assume this was a collective of work friends. Their position was one of the best spots to take in the full spectacle, though of course Noah's guardian being one of the first people on the scene, and privy to the highest level of gossip was surely a bonus. To their credit, this mismatched group seemed to be taking the time to engage with Noah and keep him distracted.

The body unsurprisingly hung exactly where it was left.

Its bulging bloodshot eyes hauntingly stared out from the sockets, the whites now a shade of pale violet. Any remaining colour had drained from the face and gave it a sickly yellow colour like a layer of dead skin on a calloused foot. The tongue lolled slightly from the mouth and the copious amount of blood that ran from the throat had dried to an inky black.

All in all, this was the scene to be expected when a crowd of people were locked in a building against their will and herded to an area where a disfigured body gently swung like a pendulum reminding them of their own mortality.

Vanic stood at the door he had just come through and surveyed the area. The huddles of people, the sporadic benches filled with confused shoppers and the occasional lone onlookers.

He cast a glance across at Melda and Chuck, still trying to sort a semblance of order amongst the crowd, and then to Noah and the shopkeepers, *classic band name acquired*, and felt the two-way pull causing internal conflict. He knew that he should go and assist with putting order to this chaos but in his mind's eye he could see Sarah's eyes burning into his skull at the very notion of not attaching himself to Noah's hip for the duration.

Careful deliberation in play he plotted a course over to Noah. He could check in and then go on to help as needed while keeping him in eyeline. That was a fair compromise he thought, plus he himself didn't exactly want to let Noah out of his sight anyway.

As he approached, the circle parted like teenagers caught huddled round a dirty magazine and greeted him with a series of nervous looking smiles.

"Hey buddy, you doing alright?" he said as he scratched behind his right ear and followed it down across under his chin as he spoke, feeling slightly awkward. This kind of felt like sitting down to teach him about the birds and the bees.

His too-big eyes lit up as he turned from the attention he was getting from the group. "I'm doing ok. Russel was showing me magic."

The portly guy in kitchen attire with mousey brown hair and matching beard, complete with a silver stud peeking through below his lower lip, reddened at this and held up a coin between his thumb and finger with a nervous grin.

"Just a little bit of sleight of hand my dude." He seemed to stumble over his words a little. "Just trying to keep the little guy's attention you know?" His head and eyes cocked in unison towards the hanging corpse.

"No, I appreciate it. Russel, was it?" Vanic offered his hand and shook it with a firm grip. Up close he could smell the fast-food aroma radiating from him.

"And of course, I must thank you too," he said as he turned to the umbral clerk that had served as babysitter up to this point. He was now stood with the girl from behind the counter in the store. It didn't look like her mood had shifted any.

The man also shook his hand. It was such a strange feeling, like shaking hands with a leather glove that had been left in the refrigerator. Not cold but cool to the touch and while not rigid, it had less give than human flesh.

"Not at all," he said with that gravelly undertone drawing through. "I have to say I was concerned when you ran off, but I quickly got the measure of it and filled in the blanks. More than happy to help."

"Well, like I say, its appreciated." He released his grip and forced a smile. "It's Vanic, by the way and I'm sure Noah's introduced himself already."

The smile in reciprocation was full of unsettling jagged black teeth. "Teorre." He tapped his name badge again with a taloned finger. "That he has."

Vanic dropped to a knee as he turned again to Noah and placed his hands gently on his shoulders.

"Hey buddy, I'm going to have to do some Dad stuff now if that's ok. I know it's a bit scary, but if you can stay here with your new friends for a little bit, I'll get right back to you, and we can get you home to Mom pretty soon alright?"

To his credit, Noah seemed to be taking the presence of a swinging corpse not far from his line of sight pretty well, and Vanic was feeling positive about the idea of avoiding years of therapy bills in the future.

"That's ok. Do you have to catch a bad man?" he asked pulling a serious, yet comical for a child, face.

"Not me on my own, but yeah that's plan." He winked as he stood up and ruffled Noah's hair.

As he made his way over to where Melda and Chuck were, he could see that any attempt to diffuse the situation with the cluster of women was evidently failing.

Stepping up to Melda he saw the immediate stink-eye from the ringleader lock onto him.

Cutting herself off mid tirade she turned to face him, hands on her hips, pushing her chest out as if to point her much strangled tits right at him.

"Can I help you?" She spat with a look of utter disgust at the sheer audacity that someone might try to interrupt her rant.

Vanic took in a slow dramatic breath before blowing it out the left side of his mouth.

"I don't know. Can you?" he paused for effect.

"Do you happen to have any relevant information on the body that's currently hanging behind us? Because if not I think it might be best if you go back on over to your pack and wait for some further updates when we have them."

He could see the rage on her face building and knew full well he was about to get very wet from an incoming shower of spittle as she lost it. This was perhaps softened by the fact he could see Melda struggling hard to contain a smirk, and Chuck absolutely failing in that respect, his face a massive grin.

"Who…who the hell do you think you are?" her response bringing the expected oral waterworks.

"Detective Vanic Bradley," he replied, wiping a droplet of liquid from his cheek with a thumb. "To my current knowledge, the only member of law enforcement currently in the building."

She was, for the first time, stumped.

"As I was saying, Ms Verallon here is currently helping me with my investigation while we wait for my colleagues to arrive. So, if you could go on back to your friends and tell them to stay close to this area until further notice, that would be great."

While he took immense pleasure in putting people like this in their place, he was fully aware that though silenced with his response, she was most likely off to her group to announce the update of a police officer on site as her gathered gossip that only she, as self-imposed spokesperson of the group could have gathered.

Regardless, Melda looked both impressed and thankful for the assistance.

"Do you think you could go round the whole building and do that for me?" she smirked. "It would certainly save me a lot of hassle."

"How about you just point anyone difficult in my direction and I'll tell them to shut the fuck up?"

"That would work too I suppose."

She was over the initial shock of the situation and to Vanic's surprise, she really didn't seem as stuck up as he had initially thought.

"Anyway, I've spoken to the chief and they're on their way over now. We're going to need someone near a phone to know when they arrive though. I think Chuck, you might be best fitted for that as you're still armed. Ideally, I'd like not to have people wandering off on their own right now."

Chuck cleared his throat and corrected his posture at this as he checked his hip to make sure he was in fact still armed.

"Yeah, I can do that. The office is close enough that I can come running if anyone shouts, I'd say."

Vanic gave him a gentle pat on the shoulder.

"That's solid thinking. You're a man of action. I like that. Just wait for the call and we can go from there. I assume it's possible to open just one of the exits?"

"Yes, we can adjust it to open just one exit pretty easily." Melda said as she gave a nod to Chuck, who then headed off in the direction of her office.

"Great. In the meantime, it's not ideal but I want to move the body and get it out of everyone's line of sight. I don't think it's really helping people relax."

"I thought it wasn't a good idea to tamper with *a crime scene?*"

He had considered this already at length.

"It's not, you're right. But I really think for everyone here it's sort of a necessity as well as for the poor guy's dignity. Pulling him up onto the walkway will most likely contaminate evidence less than trying to cover him where he is."

"You're the boss. Let's get to it then."

"You don't have to, I'm sure I can find someone to give me a hand."

She let out a sigh and cocked her head as she gave him the blankest of expressions.

"Yes, very chivalrous. You realise that I am likely stronger than you, right? And I don't really want anyone having to be more involved than they need to. So, like I said, let's get to it."

He started to reply and immediately thought better of it. It had never really occurred to him before now, but he seemed to have a wonderful ability to surround himself with some of the strongest willed, independent women on the planet.

"Fine. Let's get this done." He sighed. "Where was all this sass when you were dealing with that dragon over there?"

CHAPTER SIXTEEN

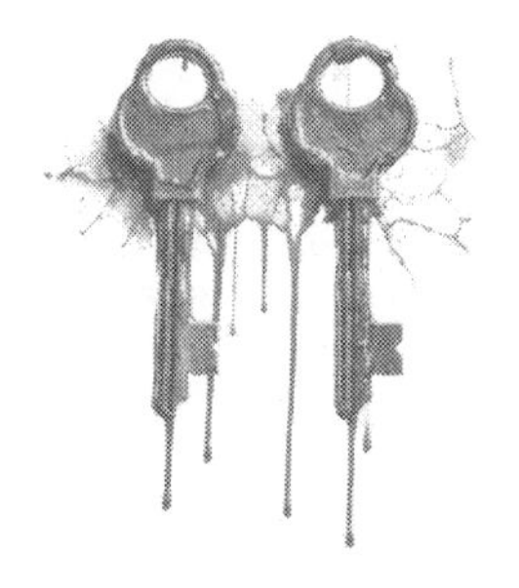

The body came over the side of the railing with a solid thud.

There was no good way to hoist up a hanging corpse by hand, but the way the body slowly flopped backwards over the rail, shoulders first as the arms hung lifeless on this side of the walkway waiting for the rest of the torso to arrive was unsettling. The way the legs folded at the knees almost hooking the body onto the railing was worse.

With a final pull, the legs came over and dropped its entire weight onto the ground. Blood had slicked its way across the top of the rail and down the inside barrier leaving a nightmare trail of crimson in its wake.

Vanic took the time to manoeuvre the body parallel along the walkway, so it was out of the way, trying his best to disrupt it as little as possible. Protocol be damned, this man's dignity was more important than his slightly disrupting a crime scene. With that in mind, he decided to check for identification.

A wallet, complete with drivers' licence, gave the victim an identity. *Calvin Thorpe.*

Vanic's stomach dropped as he felt a prickly chill run over his body as a wave of guilt hit him. He stared at the tiny picture on the ID, a much different, more alive, face staring back at him. *Calvin, are you dead because of me?*

He took a moment to catch his breath and looked over the walkway at the collective of onlookers that had been watching them work, the mixed emotions visible on their faces. There was always a small percentage of ghouls that seemed to revel at the sight of such horrific situations, and it made him sick to his stomach.

Melda seemed to be taking things in her stride now and Vanic found himself surprised at a level of respect he was suddenly feeling for her.

"How are you holding up?" he asked as he wiped his hands on the backs of his thighs.

She looked momentarily lost in thought but quickly snapped out of it. "I won't say this is the best day I've had in work, that's for sure." She gave the body on the ground a cursory glance. "But honestly, I'm doing ok. Thank you."

He nodded slowly while he took her in.

The very nature of his job had him crossing paths with members of the umbral community on a nightly basis and it was rarely in a positive light. Josh always joked about how he had a jaded worldview of them as a result and the infuriating nickname he had picked up on the streets didn't exactly help that.

Lamplighter.

A person employed to light and maintain the candles in streetlights. To 'ward off the darkness' so to speak. He didn't think he went any harder on any particular person, regardless of race. A perp was a perp, perhaps umbral guys just put up more of a fight.

Standing here, taking in this woman who was likely not only seeing a dead body for the first time but had just helped to hoist it up over the walkway, he was really starting to question his bias.

"You're doing great. Honestly." He scratched at his jaw again. "Which is why I feel bad asking for more of you, but you're honestly the closest thing I've got to a partner in here."

"Look, I appreciate you buttering me up but if you think I'm going to assist in an autopsy you're dead wrong." She said with a smirk.

Vanic laughed for what felt like the first time in forever. "No, no, I think we're good on that point." He glanced down over the railing at the crowd. "I need to do a full perimeter check of the building while we're waiting though, and I would really appreciate it if you could get a headcount of everyone down there. It would make sorting suspects a little easier once the cavalry arrives."

She placed both her hands on the top of the railing as she too looked over the side at the crowd gathered below, her pointed fingers gripping tightly on the barrier. "Sure."

She said without looking back at him. "Admin work. Admin work I can handle."

"It'd be a massive help. If anyone seems shifty, obviously feel free to make a note of that too." He hesitated for a second before continuing. "Sensitive topic but do I need to point out the obvious here?"

At this she turned from the crowd and gave him a puzzled look, one eyebrow raised in an almost comedic manner. "The obvious?" She asked.

His jaw tightened and he felt himself go rigid, the playfulness they had casually adopted melting away. "You've seen the bodies. Those injuries. The suspect, or suspects are mostly likely umbral."

"Oh." Her face immediately fell into a grimace. "I hadn't really stopped to consider that at all. Now that you've pointed it out though, I guess that does make sense."

"It's nothing that really needs to concern you, just a point of note," he said, happy to move the conversation on. "Can you give me a rundown of how many corridors I need to check?"

She quickly did a mental map of the building.

"So, there are four doors on each side, on each floor. The first two loop back on each other and are the same for the floor above, connected by the staircase at the back. The back half of the mall is a repeat of the same layout. The back two on the west side also lead through to the warehouse and loading dock."

"Ok, so two loops each side and repeat for upstairs. That's not so bad. Thank you. I'll let you get back downstairs and make a start on this far end with the loading dock and check that's secure first."

They both headed back down the stairs to the waiting onlookers in the main body of the mall and he watched as Melda rushed off to make a start on her headcount.

He drew in a deep breath, filling his lungs and slowly exhaled as he looked over to where Noah was still enthralled by his new friends and waited to catch his attention. After a few seconds, they made eye contact and he threw him a thumbs up with a smile, which Noah quickly returned before he went back to focusing on whatever the big guy, *Russel was it,* was doing.

After spending a moment to decide whether it was worth grabbing the pistol from Chuck, he reasoned that he would feel more comfortable knowing someone here was armed, should they need to be and readied himself to start his sweep of the mall.

Barely a few steps in, that plan was already on hold as a man began to approach from the crowd. Pointed ears protruded through his fiery short locks and though he looked to be in his early twenties, elven blood made that almost a wild guess. He approached with a casual saunter, his rust-coloured sneakers, charcoal skinny jeans, black t-shirt and what looked to be the love child of a blazer and a cut off denim jacket over the top, were a fashion statement Vanic couldn't fathom.

Vanic was pretty sure this was the kid that had been filming the body with his phone earlier and he prepared himself for a difficult encounter.

"Hey, yo. I'm glad I caught you." He said as he closed the gap.

"Is there something I can help you with?" Vanic really wasn't in the mood to deal with some punk looking for gory details.

The kid adjusted his jacket at the break line with both hands and Vanic noticed the obvious bulge in the upper pocket. A reporter perhaps.

"Maybe," he said as he ran his fingers through his hair. "It's looking to me like you're sort of running the show here?"

"Firstly, how about you stop the recording on your phone, and we can go from there." He nodded to the man's breast pocket.

he gave a smirk before reaching in and drawing the phone out, hitting the display on the front and turning the phone to Vanic in an open gesture to show he had done just that.

"Sorry, you just don't get a lot of chances to witness this kind of thing, seems a shame not to document it."

"This is a crime scene and a death, not a solar eclipse. You might want to consider that before you act like it's something to celebrate." He was sure the glare he was giving the kid wasn't going unnoticed either. "Plus, people might like to be informed before you try and record them."

"Yeah, you're right. I'm sorry. Let's start this again. The names Rith," he said and held out his hand.

Vanic shook his hand, squeezing a little harder than necessary. "Rith?"

"Well, Irithiel, but that's a bit formal really."

"Vanic Bradley," he said. "And to answer your question, no I'm not running anything. I just appear to be the only member of law enforcement in the building right now, so just doing what I can until they arrive. Which I can assure you will be quite soon."

"I just meant in so much as someone taking the lead sorry." Both hands raised in a gesture of surrender. "Law enforcement… so that would make you a detective?"

The word landed with the intent it was obviously supposed to and Vanic cursed inwardly. He didn't like the idea of anyone connecting the dots the same way he had but it also further added to the theory that he was working with.

'*Welcome Detective.*'

Could this whole thing be for his benefit? And if so, why was he being targeted? He was sure he didn't know the victim and the lengths that someone must have gone through to plan this were insane. This gave thought to a more worrying idea. What was the end goal?

"It wouldn't necessarily make me a detective, but in this case that would be correct yes." He wanted this conversation over with.

"Sorry again, I didn't mean to make any assumptions, it's just you know," and he pointed to where the body formerly hung. "The sign."

"I don't think we can really assume what any of this means at this point. I think its best we just hang on until the people equipped to find out get here."

"Yeah of course." He had a look of losing interest about him now. "It's just, like you said, you're the only detective here."

Vanic was done with this conversation.

"We don't know who it was for, maybe it was for when the police arrived. Like I say, its best if everyone stay put and stick together until they arrive."

And with that, Vanic exited the conversation and made his way across the mall towards the first door on his list.

Upon reaching the door, he paused for a second to look back at the crowd and saw Rith now bothering a couple sat on a bench. That one might potentially be a problem if reinforcements don't get here soon.

He sighed again and opened the door, ready to begin his search.

He felt the anxiety inside him bubbling to the surface, things felt wrong. He was starting to regret not calling Roma, her objections aside, it would be nice to hear her voice right now. He even considered Josh, though he wasn't sure what he'd have to say to him right now.

CHAPTER SEVENTEEN

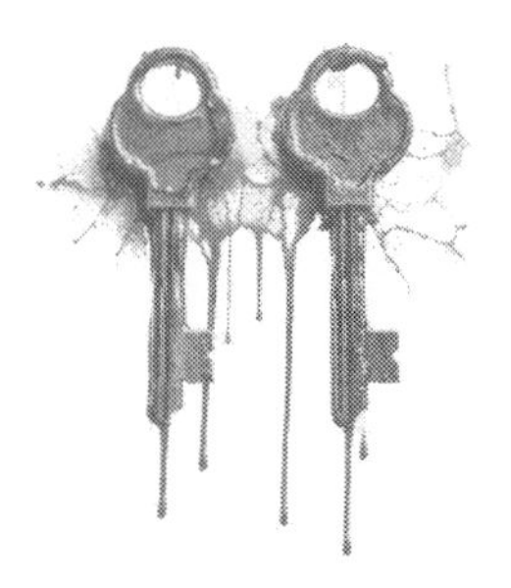

In hindsight, searching the hidden rooms and corridors unarmed and alone was probably a stupid plan but he still didn't like the idea of leaving the group and especially his son, alone without some form of protector. The fact that Chuck was the only one with a gun was bad enough but knowing he was still a corridor away from the crowd wasn't ideal.

None of this was ideal.

The only silver lining so far being that he had managed to loop the whole of the first back section of the mall, both upper and lower floors including the warehouse and loading bay, without issue. He had confirmed there was no way to escape through the loading dock and having checked out the whole warehouse area as well as the offices and staff rooms along the way, could confirm there was nobody hiding in this section.

He had a couple of times heard noises that had startled him but upon checking them out, came up with nothing. It was true that without someone monitoring the exits, he couldn't fully be sure someone wasn't cleverly sneaking around him, but a proper search could be carried out when everyone else arrived.

There wasn't a chance in hell he would be leaving though. If this wasn't some sort of massive coincidence, then he was being targeted and he needed to be here to see things through to the end. If this was someone with a vendetta against him, then all these people were trapped inside the mall because of him, when they could be safe at home with their loved ones.

As he headed back out into the main body of the mall ready to make a start on the next section, he was aware of a new level of commotion. The very energy of the hall was different, a palpable buzz of anticipation.

Melda was stood at the far door on the other side of the mall talking to Chuck and when her eyes locked with his, she waved for his attention.

Hopefully it's a positive update, he thought as he made a quick beeline across the mall towards her.

She had an almost manic look on her face and Chuck was grinning as he approached.

"They're outside now," she said, flustered like a lovestruck teen waiting to meet the latest pop icon. 'They said to open just the entrance they're at as soon as we could. Looks like you've timed it well.'

He could feel the tension melting away immediately with the knowledge he could soon get Noah back to his mom and start a more organised and methodical breakdown of events. He could clearly see Noah diving into Sarahs waiting arms, the relief visible on her face. He also longed to see Roma. To be able to recount this whole ordeal like a footnote in life, and not a living nightmare.

"Right, let's get this show on the road then. Shall we?" he said as he gestured past himself towards the direction of the control panel they had earlier visited.

They made their way over to the panel, with Melda giving the occasional reassurance as members of the crowd stepped forward, clearly aware of events in motion. Chuck kept pace with Vanic, and they soon made it to the box and unlocked it as they waited for Melda to catch up.

She wasn't too far behind and once she arrived gave Chuck the nod to proceed. 'Ok Charles, let's not keep the nice officers waiting.'

There was a whole series of dials and switches on the console and Vanic watched as Chuck inserted the key into the middle slot of three spaces in a recess on the left of the panel and gave it a turn.

Nothing happened.

There was an awkward passage of a few seconds before Chuck righted the key in the slot and tried it again with the same outcome.

"So, is there supposed to be a sound or alert here?" Vanic asked.

"Let me try." Melda gently pushed Chuck out of the way and inserted her key into the same slot.

Once.

Twice.

Three times she tried to no avail before she withdrew the key and tried the space above. Still nothing. She tried the bottom slot a couple of times as the frustration on her face began to spread into visible panic.

Finally, she removed the key and re-inserted it into a slot on the right side of the console and gave it a turn. There was an audible buzz from the panel, and she began to turn one of the dials on the display. The lighting in the mall began to dim and brighten around them as she rotated the dial. Another dial then adjusted the volume of the now tedious background soundtrack that was being looped through the building.

"I don't understand," she said as she once again tried the initial space on the left of the panel to no success. Worry was beginning to show on her face, the cracks in her stoic mask of control starting to become apparent.

"I appear to have full control of the building except for the doors." She was visibly panicking now.

A wave of dread washed over Vanic. The pieces were starting to fall together in a way that he really didn't like. There was something far more calculated and sinister afoot and he was really beginning to feel the panic of isolation set in, his palms felt slick with sweat and his heart was making its best attempts to burst from his chest. Was this some sort of cat and mouse game that he was now unwillingly caught up in, and if so, why him?

"Keep trying. I'm going to run to the phone and update them on the outside." He spun on his heels and made off towards the other door for Melda's office.

Inside her office he paused to catch his breath and then punched the button to return the last call. Four rings and it was answered.

"Hello." The chief answered from the other end of the line.

"Chief, its Vanic. The doors aren't opening."

There was a brief pause. "Well, that's going to be a bit of a problem isn't it."

"A problem for your side of the doors it would seem. I don't think there a whole lot we can do from in here."

A frustrated and audible sigh filled the earpiece. "I'll see what we can do about overriding the locks from outside but failing that we're going to have to cut through and I'll be honest with you Van, that won't be quick."

"I don't doubt it." He said. "Chief, I don't think this is a coincidence. I'm pretty sure whoever is in here knows exactly what he's doing."

"Well, if he makes an appearance, be sure to ask him for me."

"I'll be sure to play twenty questions while I'm chasing him down."

At that a thought occurred to him. Something definitive that he could at least follow up on and gets some solid, though concerning answers.

"I need you to do something else for me too. Can you contact the mayor and ask if he arranged zoo tickets for me?"

"Is this really the time to be planning a day trip?"

"No, that's why I'm here. If he didn't, then I think my gut feeling is right and this whole thing is for my benefit."

"Oh. Not ideal. Would you care to elaborate on that?"

Vanic paused to consider how best to summarise his thoughts before he continued. "The Umbral that escaped the raid recently. I'm sure you read the report, he got all up in my business before he fled. If that guy was in charge, who knows what connections he's got."

"Ok, I'll see what I can do on every front and get back to you. Try to keep everyone calm and together while we work things out."

The line went dead as he ended the call.

Vanic replaced the receiver and sat in the desk chair, head in his hands, a world of scenarios running through his mind. He didn't think he had any enemies. Sure, he had built up a solid reputation for taking criminals down and yes that had garnered the unfortunate nickname on the streets but that didn't equate to some sort of nemesis.

His gut told him this was the guy who had threatened him outside the warehouse, but if he took every threat he'd received from criminals to heart, he'd have hundreds of people gunning for him. In fact, he routinely dealt with low level criminality. Thugs, thieves, and bottom tier drug dealers. There wasn't a single person he could think of that would go to the lengths of something like this. Murder and complete containment of a whole mall was certainly beyond the scope of most people he'd dealt with and that was before even factoring in the details of his own identity.

Regardless of all of that though, he was pretty sure the chief was going to confirm that mayor Farnham didn't send the tickets and that he had in fact been herded here step by step by someone with a much bigger plan. A plan he was still completely in the dark about.

He could feel the frustration bubbling to the surface and was beginning to let the sense of feeling utterly powerless get to him. Jaw clenched, he swiped out with his arm and send a mug flying off the desk and into the wall, shattering it on impact. *Great job, idiot. That will teach the mug a lesson.*

CHAPTER EIGHTEEN

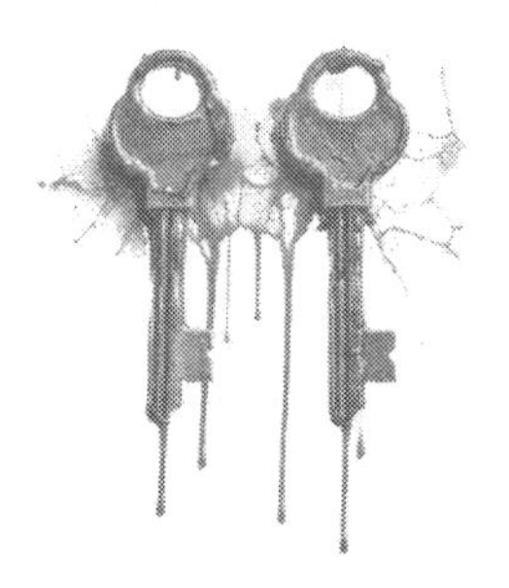

Stepping back out into the mall, Vanic quickly crossed back over to where Chuck and Melda were still tinkering with the control panel. There was now a large dent caved into the upper portion of the console above the central dials and he instinctively cocked an eyebrow at Chuck.

"I, erm, well… I got frustrated." He coughed, looking guilty.

"Still no joy then I assume?"

"No, it does appear it's just the doors, but there's nothing we can do about it," Melda said, appearing to finally give up with the key.

"It's ok, I've told them as much and they're going to see what they can do from outside and take it from there."

“Where does that leave us for now then?” she asked as she locked the panel and ran her palms down the sides of her clothes, smoothing herself out.

Pretty much exactly where we are at the moment unfortunately.” He said with an exaggerated shrug. “How did you get on with a headcount?”

She pulled out her phone and flicked up on the screen before opening a page of notes.

“One hundred and seventy-nine people,” she said quickly. “Sixty-two various members of staff and one hundred and seventeen others.”

Vanic tried to find a positive in that number. It was a lot of people, but this could have been much worse if it hadn’t happened right before closing time. He pictured five times that number being locked in here and had to stop himself, to keep calm and prevent his mind from spiralling out of control.

As he was about to thank her, she continued over him.

“Thirty-seven umbral, eleven elves, twenty-three dwarves and one hundred and eight humans. All in, we have five children present, including your son. All humans.”

He gave her a stare as he realised his jaw would need picking up off the floor.

“That is,’ He paused to consider. ‘Incredibly thorough. Thank you.”

She gave him a blank look that showed she obviously didn’t consider this to be anything more than routine and continued.

“I can give you headcount of both male and female numbers too if you think that’s relevant?”

"No. That's great honestly. You're being a massive help."

He squatted down with his back to the cool wall and looked around at the clusters of people still milling about in groups and weighed up what his next step should be.

The mall served as a throughway for Fallowport, via the underground and Vanic knew that those sealed doors were Incredibly industrial for a reason. The deep seeded prejudice that still lived in the minds of many people wasn't exactly a closely guarded secret. Even with years of work and an ungodly amount of money spent on working towards full integration of the umbral community, it was no surprise that fail safes to contain and limit access were in place. Bottom line, those doors weren't going to be a quick blowtorch job to get open.

With this knowledge in mind, he was having to face facts that there was a possible likelihood that they could be in here for days. His thoughts flashed to Noah and the other children. There was only so long before composure began to slip, and they would pick up on fear that was growing in the crowd. *What sort of toll would this take on them?*

He started to run through all the necessary elements of dealing with a contained group of nearly two hundred people being held hostage within the building. The very thought of this was as anxiety inducing as the idea of the killer on the loose with them.

People overall aren't unreasonable for the most part. Crowds on the other hand, they were a problem. The more people you add to a group, the worse the herd mentality is, and the chance of issues grows exponentially.

Vanic certainly didn't need a riot on his hands right now, especially with a murderer potentially hiding somewhere in the building.

He dropped onto his ass and splayed his legs out in front of him as he started to count off the measures he needed to put into place.

Food. He said to himself as he flicked his thumb into the air. Keeping the people fed was very much the easiest way to keep people happy. Given the existence of the food court, food itself wasn't going to be a problem but he would have to ask Melda if some of the staff could man the stations. They would have to set up allotted times for eating and limit the availability for sure. Reassuring the staff that they would be paid and the crowd themselves that it would be free, should deal with most issues. Tell them to look at it like being fed on vacation, he thought.

Next was sleeping arrangements, that would be trickier. He didn't think there was going to be any good way to make that work. They could likely source something that would work for the kids, but the adults were basically on the ground. He would again have to speak to Melda about arranging a time that the lights could be dimmed to at least give the illusion of night-time.

Those were the main concerns he would have to deal with he thought. He considered the idea of telling people to use the bathroom in groups but that seemed like it would add more fuel to the fire and have people panicking, so he shelved that idea as quickly as he had it. On top of this, he knew he would have to go around the crowd and fill everyone in on the situation as it stands and deal with an inevitable barrage of questions he likely couldn't answer. Perhaps he could get Melda to organise a time when he could give a blanket announcement to the crowd.

On top of this, the idea that the killer, or killers, could be masquerading as anyone in this crowd, hiding in plain sight, was weighing heavy on his mind.

Moreover, he still had to give the rest of the building a thorough search and keep in communication with the guys outside. Add to this the fact he needed to maintain his role as parent and spend some time with Noah, his workload was certainly piling up.

The tell-tale dull throb beginning to make an appearance behind his eyes was a sign that he was going to have to add tracking down some painkillers to that list and the need for a cigarette was building up inside him.

Smoking, another concern to add to the list, though given the circumstances he decided it was easier to let that one slide and perhaps just tell people to be mindful of it and dispose of the butts carefully.

Heaving himself up off the ground with a groan he decided it was best not to waste too much time sitting around and that if he was going to be in for a long stretch with things, he would feel much more comfortable knowing he had at least given the whole area a quick once over.

He would check in again with Noah briefly first, the sharp pangs of guilt reminding him that his son was part of this, then give Melda an update on his thoughts and have her get the ball rolling on that before continuing with his search. He hadn't fully decided if he wanted to find who they were looking for and whether he was prepared for how that would pan out.

A COUPLE OF HOURS LATER HE HAD COMPLETED A FULL search of the building, which had turned out to be worryingly uneventful. There was no sign of anyone in the remaining areas hidden away behind closed doors, which left him three possibilities. He was missing something and there were more places to hide than he thought, the person or persons was creeping about around him, or whoever it was had managed to seamlessly slip into the crowd of gathered people.

There wasn't exactly a favourable outcome amongst them, but Vanic figured that hiding in plain sight was probably the worst of the three.

He had managed to find time to check in with Melda, who continued to be her ever impressive self and had already organised an evening meal for the whole group; Burgers and fries, keeping it simple.

He had also found the time to check back in with the chief, which had yielded yet more bad news. Nobody seemed to have any ideas on how to override the doors controls from the outside, and so breaking through was looking more likely to be the sadly time-consuming plan of action.

More worrying, yet unsurprisingly it appeared that the mayor had absolutely no idea about the tickets he had received, and this confirmed the horrible gut feeling Van had been harbouring since everything had kicked off.

This whole situation had been meticulously planned out for him alone. Someone had taken the time to carefully lure him to the mall and almost literally dropped a body in his lap. They had expected his immediate lockdown response and been one step ahead with severing any surveillance or chance of escape. The plan had already left three bodies in its wake, and it was entirely unsurprising that he couldn't track down whoever was behind this as they had clearly planned this all out ahead of time.

Presently the biggest concern wasn't why? Although that was high on the list; it was *what next?* Someone had gone to great lengths to set all this up and the most worrying thing about it was that they obviously weren't done yet.

With all these thoughts running through his mind, Vanic did his best to push them down and focus on the present. It was starting to get late and there wasn't a whole lot else he could do right now, so he decided it was time to speak with Melda again about organising an announcement and making the necessary arrangements for sleep. He also wanted to spend some time with Noah before settling him down for the night.

CHAPTER NINETEEN

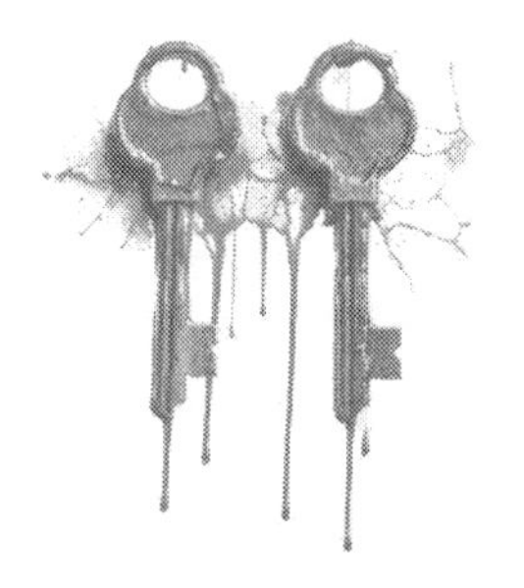

The next couple of hours passed swiftly, though they weren't entirely uneventful.

Melda had once again done her part and organised a platform for Vanic to give a crowd wide update of what was going on for the gathered party. He wasn't the best public speaker and tried to keep things succinct and swift.

He was surprised that the information, negative as it was, had been received with relative calm and minimal outrage. The level of panic and the unknown that everyone was already dealing with probably helped to soften the blow of bad news and presumably having some form of update on their forced captivity, played a part as well.

He was entirely unsurprised that, as minimal as it was, what shouts and cries of outrage he did receive, were entirely human. Most of the crowd seemed to accept their situation in this predicament well enough, but there would always be the few that considered their rights were being infringed on, as if this was his doing and he could do anything about it.

Overall, to walk away without a full-blown riot on his hands, or at the very least something big and heavy being thrown at his head, he considered this a relative success.

The group had then set off to make what arrangements they could to sort some kind of sleeping set up.

Various cushions were taken from seats in the stores and a few padded pieces of furniture that mostly served as the limbo area for boyfriends and husbands to gather while they waited for their significant others to conclude their shopping trips, were dragged out into the main hall. This didn't provide a lot of comfort but would be enough to provide bedding for the children present.

Vanic assumed that given he had held back a possible timeframe from the group, that most of the adults were likely to try and stay awake throughout the night anyway. A problem to be considered should his thoughts be correct, and the situation wouldn't be resolved overnight.

The overhead lights had shortly after been dimmed by Melda. They had settled on a comfortable level of darkness. Dim enough to be considered night, but not to the point that people would have to resort to clumsily feeling around in the dark. It reminded Vanic of the occasional weekends from his childhood when he and his father would go camping in the woods, the all-encompassing blackness lifted to a cool blue-purple hue against the moonlight.

Vanic sat with his back against the wall as he watched over Noah, curled up in the foetal position on the long grey cushioned stool that had been sourced from a shoe store.

From his position he could see the groups of people scattered about in the cliques they had formed, trying to make themselves comfortable in the dark. It unnerved him that the few umbral residents blended almost seamlessly into the darkness, but that couldn't really be helped. He also couldn't miss the stares that were occasionally being shot his way, quickly followed up with the hushed whispers he couldn't make out. The seeds of mistrust planting themselves in his mind.

Further along from where he was sat, a dwarven man with a bald head and a full chestnut brown beard flowing down to his stomach was lay against the wall with his legs splayed out before him, head resting on the bin to his left, snoring rhythmically. It seemed the concept of being trapped against their will wasn't an issue for everyone.

The subtle odour of grilled meats and grease from this evening's meal were still hanging in the air and he felt his stomach churning as it growled at him. He would have to make sure he didn't miss whatever would be planned for breakfast.

Vanic placed a relaxed fist on the top of Noah's sleeping head and slowly fanned his fingers out, letting them brush through his hair before repeating the process, the warmth from his sons' scalp was oddly comforting and he found himself lost in thought as he carried on gently stroking him and allowed his own head to rest back against the wall and closed his eyes.

THE PLASTIC TRAY WAS THE ONLY THING BETWEEN HIS CHIN and the solid ground, though it still didn't provide a great deal of protection as he hit the floor, food cascading up around him like tiny cuisine fireworks.

His teeth clacked together as he hit the ground and it was only his quick reflexes in dropping the tray and thrusting his palms out at the approaching floor that stopped him doing greater damage to his face.

The background chatter of the school canteen died instantly as he landed, like some higher power had hit the pause button on the room for a moment. What felt like an eternity, though was likely only a couple seconds, passed before the hall erupted into a cacophonous roar of cheers and laughter as the children around the room started up again.

From the corner of his eye, Van saw a black boot straighten up from the jutted position it had been in only moments before.

"Oh dear, how awful." A voice like glass on glass intoned from above him. "It looks like you've made quite the fool of yourself, Van. And quite a mess of yourself too it seems."

Vanic slowly picked himself up off the ground and turned to face the voice.

Stood before him were three umbral boys from his class. Front and centre with a mock look of sympathy on his face was a boy in a blue hoodie, his hand outstretched offering a white napkin. He was flanked either side by two larger framed boys, both in grey sweatshirts. One sported relatively short thorny spikes of hair, while the other had longer tendrils of darkness that fell to his shoulders. Both had broad vicious grins on their faces.

"It's not exactly conducive to making friends you know. Making a frankly idiotic spectacle of yourself that is." He raised the offered napkin to his own lips and blotted at the side of his mouth. "Wouldn't you say so, Karn?"

"Quite the opposite I'd say," said the boy with the longer hair.

Vanic could taste the metallic tang of blood in his mouth and the inside of his lower lip felt coarse against his tongue.

"You tripped me!" he said as he was trying his best to hold back the tears welling in his eyes as his cheeks reddened.

The boy in blue looked aghast in fake horror as he replied. "Me? Well, that couldn't possibly be the case. We're stood very much out of the way here I can assure you."

"Completely out of the way," the third boy finally chimed in.

Vanic could feel the rage building up inside him and he was doing his best to try to push it back down. His eyes were glassy and there was a lump in his throat that he knew would betray him if he opened his mouth again.

He knelt to pick up his tray, though its contents were now spread across the floor with the rest still clinging to his own clothing and stood back up with it gripped firmly in both hands, the tips of his fingers going pink as he gripped so tightly.

"You're a bunch of jerks." He spat. "It doesn't matter if nobody else saw it, eventually someone won't put up with it and then you'll have to deal with the consequences."

He was impressed that his voice hadn't cracked like he had expected, and he stood his ground for a few seconds, not breaking his gaze from the ringleader.

"What an angry little outburst. Maybe you should spend a bit more time watching where you're going and less time spouting such nonsense," he said as he poked a pointed finger into Vanic's chest.

He'd had enough.

Vanic let out a feeble childlike roar as he swung the tray with both hands, the look of absolute shock appearing on the other boys' face as it hurtled towards him.

HE WOKE UP WITH A SPASM THAT SHOT THROUGH HIS WHOLE body causing an involuntary twitch of his neck.

For a moment he had forgotten where he was, and it was the discomfort in his lower back that brought him up to speed. He was still sat propped up against the wall and his right hand was resting gently on Noah's side.

Gazing around the room he remembered that they were running on artificial night, and there could be no way to tell how much time had actually passed based on the level of darkness.

He could see that there were now a lot more people assuming some attempt at sleep, or at least resting and he considered for the first time what a help that would be. A sleepy person was a cranky person, and he didn't relish the idea of tempers running high from a lack of sleep.

He wondered how they were getting on outside; it would be an around the clock situation but at least they could rotate staff.

He wondered too how Sarah was coping. This would be incredibly worrying for her, and he wouldn't be surprised if she was on the other side of those doors right now, fighting with the chief and trying to break through with her bare hands.

CHAPTER TWENTY

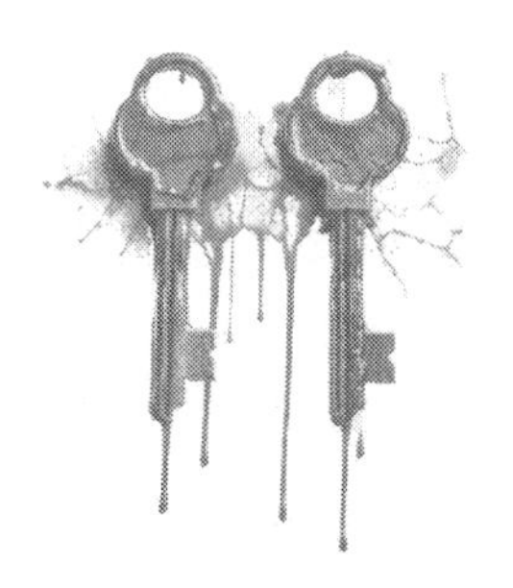

Sleep came easily but was sadly not long lasting.

Another blood curdling scream resonated through the hall and woke Vanic with a start, the way the scream carried throughout the building was a testament to the power of acoustics.

The lighting had been adjusted back to daylight levels and his first sight upon opening his eyes was several people rushing towards the direction of the scream. He checked on Noah, who had also awoken to the sound and was looking up at him with confusion in his eyes.

"It's ok, buddy." He adopted a squat in front of his son. "Just stay right here and Dad's gonna go see what's going on."

He waited for a nod and jumped up, immediately heading for the direction of the crowd. Weaving between benches and superfluous fake plastic trees, he quickly found the source of the scream and gathered crowd outside a sporting goods store.

Outdoor Adventure. A place for all your sporting needs. Balls, bats, uniforms, hiking boots and camping equipment. If you need it, they have it. The glowing white sign nacreous against the backdrop of deep blue.

Skidding to a halt on his heels, Vanic could see about a dozen people outside the store with Noah's amateur magician friend seemingly barring the entrance. The young elven guy he spoke to briefly yesterday, *Rith, was it?* was there too, alongside the bald dwarf he had shared a wall with only a few hours earlier. The rest of the crowd appeared to be a variety of men from the group that had come running at the sound of the scream. A woman, presumably the source of the scream, lay unconscious on the ground with two others tending to her.

He pushed his way through the small gathering and turned his attention to the de facto gatekeeper, who seemed instantly relieved to see him.

"Russel." Vanic said as he threw up a wave and squeezed past two men that were still trying to barge their way into the store. "Would you like to fill me in?"

Russel puffed up his cheeks and blew the air out slowly as he raised his eyebrows in a visual cue that said: "There's a lot."

Vanic spun around and raised both hands up, palms to the crowd and began to speak. "Everybody, please. If you can all just calm yourselves for a minute, that would be amazing. I fully appreciate you all rushing here to the rescue, but if I can just get a rundown of what's happened, we can go from there. Thank you."

He turned back to Russel and put an arm around his shoulder and walked them both forwards to the entrance to the store.

"So, what have I missed?" he said as he leaned in close to Russel's ear.

He hesitated for a second, as if trying to put it into words and then said simply: "I think it's going to be easier to just show you." As he led them into the store.

The inside of the store was brightly lit with fluorescent blue lighting running along the walls on both sides. Row upon row of sneakers and boots lined those walls for the first thirty to forty feet, before widening up into a mass of tables and small shelving units, heavily broken up with mannequins in sports gear and pop-up tents. The whole place smelled strongly artificial, like the plastic smell from opening a new box of sneakers. chemical and spongey.

As they walked towards the back of the store, he quickly realised what the issue was, as well as the source of both the scream and Russel's demeanour.

Vanic's stomach dropped, and his mouth went dry.

The body of a man in his thirties, with short brown hair and designer stubble was tied to a mannequin with rows of orange and yellow climbing rope wrapped around his chest. His arms hung loosely at his side and his face was coated in blood that ran from his eye sockets like a fabled weeping statue.

The blood below the lids had dried to a thick dark crust, leaving the open sockets staring like two cavernous pits of bright red tissue the color of fresh watermelon. The eyes themselves may have potentially been removed, but Vanic had a horrible feeling it was more likely that they had been pushed into the skull by force. The force of sharp clawed thumbs, he thought.

On the ground in front of the body lay a large sheet of white card, complete with writing in blood, much like the one hanging from the other body.

Arm yourself

Protect the townsfolk...

Placed carefully on the lower left and right of the card were two handguns, laid in alignment with the edges of the sign.

At this point Vanic realised that the surrounding area had clearly been adjusted for the scene and there were mannequins outfitted in war-ball helmets and shoulder armor, grasping vanquish ball bats and in one instance a compound bow and quiver.

He reached down and picked up one of the pistols and ejected the cartridge into his other hand.

Empty.

At this point Russel decided to break the silence. "What do you think it means?"

"Well, it would seem whoever is in here with us is sending a message." Vanic clicked the magazine back into the pistol and tucked it into the back of his trousers. "It looks like they're preparing for a fight and are letting us know. These, I would assume, are the two guns missing from security. Apparently, whatever they have planned, both sides are going to have to keep it close quarters."

The color drained from Russel's face, and he looked queasy. "This is insane, you know that right? What are you going to do?"

"I'm not going to go running around the mall in plastic armor and a helmet if that's what you mean. Though I think once this gets back to everyone things are going to get a lot more tense."

"No doubt." Russel said as he perched on a nearby table, pushing back a pile of folder sports shirts.

"Can you give me any insight on what happened before I got here? You were here first?"

"Second," he said. "I was up getting ready to start on breakfast for people like miss Melda had asked and I heard the scream and came running. I think he's her boyfriend or husband. Poor woman."

"Right, and there was nobody else about I assume?"

"No, I just sort of dragged her out and then people started showing up. You weren't too far behind."

"That doesn't leave us much to work with then, and this poor guy has been here a while by the look of him. I wonder..."

"Holy mother of fuck!" the voice cut Vanic off as he was speaking.

Melda was stood behind them clutching her clipboard to her chest like a new-born.

"This is getting way beyond out of hand now," she said as she waved her clipboard across the scene. "We can't just wait here expecting to be picked off one by one."

"Melda, where's Chuck?" Vanic asked in a panic.

"I told Charles not to move away from the group. It seemed like the sensible thing to do. Do you have any idea what's going on?"

"I'm in the dark as much as you, but it's not good and I think it's only just getting started."

"Well do you have a plan of action, detective?"

"Working on it," he replied honestly. "We need to get this guy down first of all, then I need to speak to his partner outside, see if she can give us any more information."

"And then?"

"Then, I need to speak to Chuck. I hate to put this on you again, but can you do another headcount? I'd like to make sure there are no more surprises waiting for me."

Vanic was expecting to hear some objections, but it seemed that the key to keeping Melda calm was to give her things to do.

"I can do that. I'm not sure I'm going to be able to keep people calm for much longer though, so I'd suggest you find a way to get us out of here pretty sharpish."

With Russel's help, they quickly untied the body and lowered it gently down behind the mannequins. Russel began grabbing shirts from the shelves and draped them over the body as Vanic started the unfortunate task of checking over the injuries.

As he had thought, the eyes had been punctured and forced into the skull, which seemed to be the only visible damage and likely cause of death. A lack of trauma to the areas around the eyes made the likelihood of a sharp implement unlikely and that thumbs were a more probably cause.

While the blood wasn't completely dry, it had been there long enough to confirm this had happened some hours earlier while it was dark.

Vanic left Russel to finish covering the corpse and stepped outside to try and get some more information from the people in the hall.

He needed to stay focused on the task at hand, but also, he needed to step away from the body as the burning guilt was beginning to eat away at him. Another life lost. *Was this his fault? How many more people would have to die because of his incompetence.*

The crowd had grown slightly larger, but thankfully not too much and the woman who had passed out earlier was now sat on a bench with a tall, athletic, blonde woman tending to her.

Vanic headed over to their bench and was taken aback by the blonde as he drew closer. She was well over six foot and as she wore a pair of Khaki shorts that came just above the knee, he could see the obvious musculature of her calves above her tan hiking boots. He took the time to take in the rest of her appearance and could see that her arms too were well built and struggling at the sleeves of her cornflower blue polo shirt. Her honey blonde hair was tied up in a ponytail and kept away from her contrasting delicate features.

He raised a polite wave as he approached. "Hi, I'm really sorry to intrude on you right now, but I really do need to ask a few questions."

The blonde looked to him as the woman on the bench also brought her head up to meet his gaze. She was brunette and while obviously tanned, her complexion was presently pale and her once pristine make-up was now smeared, with trails of charcoal streaks running from her eyes.

She spluttered a little and emitted a hoarse cough before replying. "Yes. Of course."

"Am I correct in assuming that is your partner inside?" He made sure to phrase it '*is*' and not '*was*', though he was sure she knew full well where things stood.

"Yes, my Fiancé, George." She clarified between sobs.

"You have my deepest sympathies," he said making sure to get that out of the way first. "Would you be able to tell me anything that might help piece this together? Had he wandered off alone?"

"He got up to use the bathroom in the night. I must have nodded off and when I woke up and he wasn't back, I went looking and…" she broke off into another sob as her whole body shivered as she wept, the blonde doing her best to comfort her.

"Thank you, that's all I need, I won't take up any more of your time, but again you have my condolences and I'm going to do my best to bring whoever it was to justice."

As he walked away, he was mentally cursing himself for not putting bathroom breaks in place like he thought, though it was likely safe while the area was well lit.

He could see now that Russel was back outside the store and that he and a few others, the bald dwarven guy included, were casually swinging bats in front of themselves as though testing the heft of the swing.

He hoped this wasn't going to turn into a pitchforked vigilante mob situation.

CHAPTER TWENTY-ONE

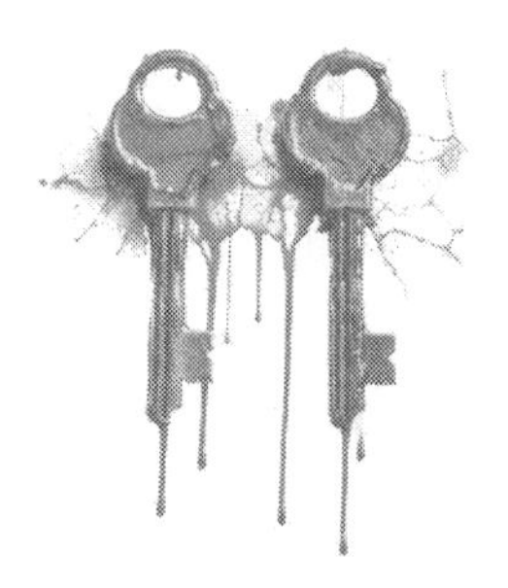

The scene back in the corridor was beyond chaos.

A few women were in hysterics, tears pouring from them freely. The scattered crowd had merged like puddles of mercury into larger clusters, and there were individual offsets of solo shoppers apparently refusing to breakdown but looking visibly distressed hovering on the side-lines.

Someone had gathered all the children together and placed them in the middle of the hall. He just wanted to be back by Noah's side, and it was killing him that he had to make this threat a higher priority. Though he reasoned that keeping everyone safe was also the best way to keep his son safe for now.

Vanic thought from up above on the second level, that the crowd's movements seemed to resemble that of amoeba through a microscope, milling about and adding to their number.

He had been stopped by three separate people on his way back to the group, all looking for information, and more unfortunately, answers. Answers that he didn't have to give.

In the time it had taken to speak with Chuck, the crowd had grown back to its original capacity, and he could see that more than a few of them were now carrying make-shift weapons from *Outdoor Adventure.* One rubenesque young man had even donned a helmet and set of shoulder guards, looking as ridiculous a hero as one would expect.

Honestly, while he didn't want this to become a mob with flaming torches, Vanic couldn't really fault the desire for the group to arm themselves. He also considered the fact that while he had to really start looking for this assailant, it was a little comfort knowing that there was more than just Chuck manning their defences, especially with Noah present.

"Chuck, I just wanted to say that I really appreciate what you're doing." Vanic said as he began adjusting his shirt, tucking it back into his trousers round the front.

Chuck looked almost bashful for a second as he cleared his throat and replied. "I'm just doing my job."

"No.' Vanic help up a palm. 'You're not. This is above and beyond your pay grade here and we both know it. Right now, in this shitstorm you are literally my only other line of defence and it's a massive weight off my shoulders to know that you're here while I'm not. I want you to know that I am incredibly grateful."

He paused and his reddening face was acceptance enough, but he continued. "Thanks. And thanks to you too, you're putting yourself in the line of fire here."

Vanic shot him a broad smile. A smile that was wholly genuine at this moment. "All in a day's work," he said. "It feels a little brighter with the odds evened slightly."

He put a hand on Chucks shoulder and gave it a gentle squeeze. "And not a word about this to anyone, yeah?" he said as he headed off in the direction of the side exit to Melda's office.

Keeping his head down as he crossed the corridor, he managed to avoid the attention of anyone else in the crowd as he made his way to the side door and headed on through it.

The acrid disinfectant smell of the floor was still strong back here and it invaded his nostrils with its harsh mix of bleach edged with lemon.

The overhead row of windows in the ceiling were now acting as thick, broad spotlights, casting a strip of circular beams of sunlight along the corridor, dust motes dancing in its rays.

Vanic found the sunlight comforting and warm as he passed through them, but it also served as a wonderful reminder that time was passing. The artificial daylight of the mall was quickly blurring the actual concept of night and day.

He took another cursory glance through the window to the door on his left as he passed.

The row of lockers lined the far wall of the staff room, presumably untouched in the past few hours. He didn't imagine a change of clothes was high on the list of priorities for the staff of the building at present. A set of crumpled clothes lay on the table to the side and spilled over onto one of the small plastic chairs. *It was a priority for someone then it seemed.*

He continued along the corridor, the brief hits of warmth as he passed under the sun granting magical moments of freedom, if only in his head, and turned the corner to Melda's office and let himself in.

The room seemed entirely untouched.

The fear gnawing away at the back of his mind was returning to another severed phone line, thus cutting off their last link to the outside. The only solid piece of intel that today's death had brought was the concrete evidence that the killer is still very much inside the building with them.

Dialling out, he got the chief after a few rings.

"Vanic, how are you holding up?"

"Well," he said. "As of this morning there's one less of us holding up. So, not great."

"Shit. Not great at all. I suppose it's too much to assume an accident?"

"Unless the poor guy accidentally put his eyes into the back of his skull and managed to then string himself up like a gift for me, I'm afraid not."

"No," he paused. "I suppose not."

"This is the part where you tell me that you've at least got some good news for me."

"I wish I could. We're having to cut our way in, but it appears these doors were built to require a lot to get through. Someone was pretty adamant on the need to prevent that it seems."

"Apparently so. And I don't suppose you're making good progress on that? It would be nice to have something positive to take back to the masses."

"Slow and steady I'm afraid. The other concern out here is that all of Fallowport on the other side are in a panic too. You're trapped in there, but from their perspective several of, their community and their loved ones are trapped."

"Wonderful. That's going to be a media sensation too then I imagine."

"Indeed. But it looks like you're going to have to carry on sitting tight while we get through this door. I trust you to take whatever measures you need to in light of this new situation. And again, no heroics Bradley."

"I think we may be past that now sir. I'll check in later."

He hung up the phone and remained sat at the desk, letting all the events so far run through his head as he tried to make any sense of it.

Someone had gone through great lengths to get him here. That same somebody now had a body count of four people under his belt and was taunting him with these messages.

The first question was why?

The second was who?

And finally, what next?

The notes seemed to imply that they wanted him to try and stop them, but if that was the case why haven't they shown themselves.

The headache from yesterday was beginning to make another appearance and he could feel that dull ache in his temples beginning to pulse as all the possible ideas swam in his mind.

Firstly, he knew that there could still only be two possible scenarios for the killer. Either they were hiding within the group, or they were somewhere else in the mall. The former being a strong worry as he was pretty sure he had covered the whole building yesterday in his search.

He could gather everyone up in one big group and make them stay together as they waited this out. if the killer was elsewhere, they wouldn't be able to pick them off that way. Toilet breaks would have to be scheduled in groups and a rotation of people acting as sentries would have to be organised too, but there was always safety in numbers.

If on the other hand, the killer was part of the group, all he could do was wait. Keeping groups to a minimum of three would at least allow the safety of nobody being left alone with a potential murderer.

The frustration was unbearable, and he decided it best to continue this train of thought back with the group, and so made his way back out into the main body of the mall.

CHAPTER TWENTY-TWO

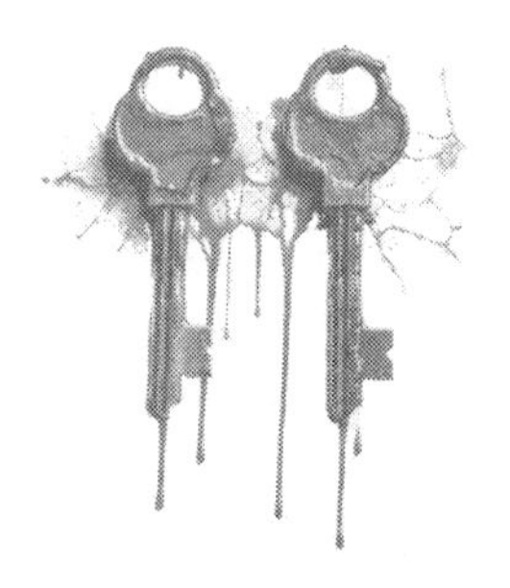

"Janine says there's a monster in the mall."

Vanic looked at Noah as he dropped this bombshell between a mouthful of fries.

"Who's Janine?"

"My friend. She said there's a monster and it's trying to get us all." He was delivering this theory with a complete lack of fear or trepidation. It was such a matter-of-fact statement between savouring his warm salty fries.

"Is Janine one of the little girls?" he asked as a he helped himself to a fry and popped it into his mouth.

"Yeah. She likes dragons and stuff. She's cool."

"Well, that's good. But no, there's no monsters in here buddy. It's just a bad man or woman and I'm here to protect you until we can get out. You don't have to worry about monsters."

At least not in the literal sense.

"Oh, ok. I wasn't worried." Again, flippant as only a child could be.

They were finishing up with their food when Vanic spotted Melda heading in their direction, the steady click-clack of her heels on the smooth floor held a pace that seemed to carry urgency.

"Sorry to interrupt. Do you have a minute?" she said calmly, though the bear-hug she was currently giving the folder in her arms alluded to a much tenser situation.

Vanic looked to the group sat in a large circle on the ground in the middle of the corridor and gave a nod to one of the men as he caught his eye.

"Noah, do you want to go and sit with the rest of the kids for a while? I just need to speak to Miss Melda."

Noah scooped up the last of his fries and palmed them into his mouth efficiently and picked up his paper plate.

"Yeah ok, don't be too long, ok?" he said as he hugged Vanic around the thigh and made his way to the group, with a detour to the nearest bin to deposit his plate.

"Shall we walk a little?" he said as he was already in motion, wanting to put a little distance between them and the group.

Once they had passed enough space to avoid keen ears, he stopped and leaned against the wall.

"Ok, shoot."

"We're a man short." She said succinctly.

Vanic raised his eyebrows but was cut off before he could speak.

"Unless I've somehow lost them in the group, which I hardly see as likely, we are one short from our head count. Male. Umbral."

"Ahh.," he said calmly. "So good and bad news then."

Melda coughed as though she had choked on her own saliva and cleared her throat.

"That's good news?" she asked as she further tightened her grip on her folder, pulling it into her chest.

"Sort of." He said as he levelled his right palm and hooked the little finger with his left hand as he began to count off.

"Firstly, it means whoever they are, they were hiding in plain sight before now. Secondly, it means that's why I couldn't find them. And thirdly…" he said as he was now squeezing three fingers in his other fist. "One person short is a much better number than anything else."

"Ok, I can see your point," she said, though she didn't seem any less tense. "What now?"

Vanic fished around in his pocket and pulled out a battered packet of cigarettes and pulled one out before offering the open packet to Melda.

She shot him a brief authoritative look.

"You know you can't smoke in….oh fuck it!" she said as she waved the folder she was holding in a grand exclamation of being past caring. "Why not."

He lit her cigarette first, before his own and took a long drag, holding the smoke in his lungs for a few seconds before exhaling with a sigh.

"Now." He took another pull. "I have to try and find this person and stop them," he said, matter-of-factly.

"Any ideas on that front?"

"Not really. They've had hours to find a foxhole to hide in. Though I'm not convinced hiding is their long-term plan."

"Suggestions?"

Like with Chuck, Vanic was again massively thankful to have Melda here with him. She had managed to become an ad hoc partner to him without even realising, and her intel so far had been particularly beneficial.

"I think I'm going to have to retrace my steps and do a corridor-by-corridor search of the whole building again. If I can convince a couple of people to come along and watch each exit this time it will give me a much more thorough sweep of the area."

"Do you think anyone is going to go for that?" She cast a glance around at the clusters of worried looking people.

"I'll only need a couple of people. I'll try the people who've decided to arm themselves first, that seems like a logical way to dig out some volunteers."

"And do you feel safe confronting whoever this is? Not that I want to tell you how to do your job, obviously."

"Safety is never guaranteed in my line of work. Precautions are really all I can rely on. But I can't afford to sit around and wait for him to strike again." He raised his leg and twisted the cigarette butt into the sole of his shoe, before placing it back into the crumpled cigarette packet.

"No objections here." She exhaled smoke through her nose in what looked a more unsettling visual than Vanic had expected.

"YOU'RE COMPLETELY SURE?" VANIC ASKED. "THERE ARE absolutely no obligations here. No shame in declining."

"Ya want me to walk behind ya like a shadow, while ya look fer a shadow. Haha!" He let out a bark of a laugh at his own joke before continuing. "I'll not be afraid confronting someone one-to-one lad. Better than sitting round being picked off unawares."

"Two to one, if it comes to that I won't be far from you at any time. Ok Jorhim, I appreciate it," Vanic said, as he took a moment to take in the muscular build of the dwarven man he had spent last night with as a wall sleeping buddy.

"Those are even better odds." He gave his bat a practise swing.

"I'll just need to find one more volunteer and we can get to it then."

A theatrical clearing of the throat drew his attention as Rith, the elven youth with the recording obsession stepped towards them.

"I'll save you the time and effort of carrying on with your search. I'm in," he said.

"Excuse me?" Vanic replied as he gave him another up and down glance.

"I've heard you asking round, and while I'm sure I'm not your first choice, I also know that you've been turned down quite a few times already. This just saves you some time."

"You're aware it could be dangerous right?"

"Firstly, I am probably older than you, so please don't treat me like a child. Secondly, sure. Only if they can get close though." He smirked as he slid a long black bow off his arm.

Vanic and Jorhim both took this in and as the dwarf opened his mouth to respond he was cut off.

"Yes, yes. An elf with a bow, I'm quite aware of the stereotype. But I will take the distance over swinging a club around aimlessly any day. Are we agreed?"

Vanic hesitated for a second and when he couldn't find a good argument for disagreeing with him, decided it was not the worst set up for what he had in mind.

"You can use that thing though, correct?"

"Well enough to hit a man-sized target should I need to, yes." His grin held a level of confidence in his abilities that was enough for Vanic.

"Fine then. If you're both sure, we might as well get on with it before it gets any later."

With that, the trio headed towards the back of the mall to begin their search, Vanic taking the lead as Jorhim fell into step alongside Rith and began pulling out every elven joke he had mentally stored away.

Vanic felt reenergised with a sense of purpose and having a plan in action, but also the trepidation of heading into a situation he couldn't fully control, with civilians in tow was causing his stomach to churn and ache like he'd received a gut punch.

CHAPTER TWENTY-THREE

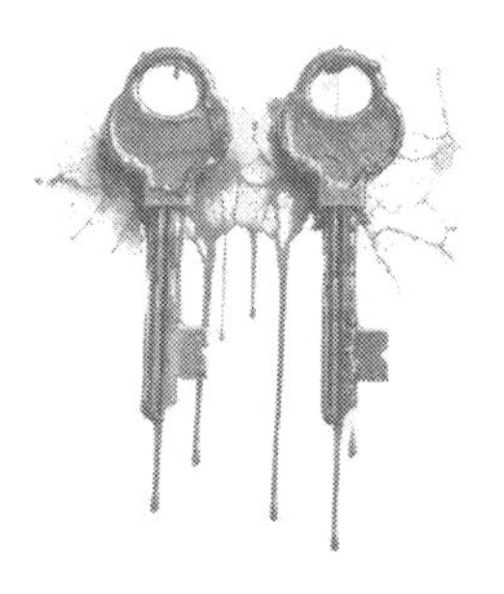

The best part of two hours later, the trio were making their way back to the group; entirely unsuccessful in their search.

Vanic had gone to lengths to make sure the plan of action was kept to by the rule. He and Jorhim would enter each section from the entrance on the ground level, the dwarf was to wait outside each room as Vanic went inside to check. This made sure that nobody could stealthily sneak past while Vanic was inside any of the rooms leading from the corridors.

Rith, meanwhile, was stationed on the upper-level door to each section, bow in hand should anyone try to leave via that point. Vanic made doubly sure to point out that they themselves would reach that door eventually and not to be too much of a hair triggered volunteer.

The whole operation was done with military precision and went off as flawlessly as he could have hoped. With the slightly more than minor issue that was not actually finding anyone.

One by one, they took each of the four areas leading off from the main area of the mall. Each time as they worked their way through the corridors and up the stairs, they were greeted by the disappointed face of Rith waiting for them.

The pounding headache that had been plaguing Vanic was showing zero signs of easing off and the sheer frustration of failing to come up with anything in the search was just tightening the metaphorical vice around his head.

"I don't know where I go from here?" he said as they carried on making their way back to the crowd.

"How so?" Rith asked as he was thankful for the break in the silence.

"I just don't have any leads. This is what I do but being here I just feel I've been handicapped from the start. I know that I'm not actually on duty here, but it's still my responsibility to do something. Four people are dead already and I'm running around with no clue what to do."

"Perhaps but consider how many might be dead if you weren't here. Do you not think that's maybe the point? That whoever this is, is playing off what you do."

"You think they've already planned for what I'm doing and they're just one step ahead? Like a game of chess?"

Rith cocked his head and gave Vanic a look that said 'think about it' before he spoke.

"Look, it's obvious this person knows all about you. Or enough to have let things play out how they have so far, so perhaps you need to start thinking of things differently too."

"Maybe you're right," Vanic said as he considered this. "I do feel like at the moment I'm just doing a really bad impression of myself."

"Then change things up. Think outside the box, go rogue, a list of other motivational statements that serve no purpose than to plaster across a poster."

Vanic stopped in his tracks and stared at him.

"What?" he said with a smirk. "Do you want me to hold your hand all the way with this?"

A couple of seconds passed in silence and then Jorhim barrelled into them with his arms outstretched, pushing them forward like a snowplough.

"Just kiss or get bloody moving alright?" he said as he pushed forward with them. "I'm starving here, and I don't think that kid is going to keep making food all night."

At that, they all burst into laughter.

"Remind me never to get on your bad side when you're hungry, Jorhim," Vanic said and for just a moment, he felt the tension easing in him. This was still far from an ideal situation, but things can always be worse.

AS THEY ARRIVED BACK AT THE CROWD, THINGS WERE WORSE.

What had been a collective of people in groups milling about calmly or in some cases still stricken with the fear of their current predicament, was now reminiscent of an early morning chat show.

While there was still a good amount of people stood around on the side-lines, their expressions were of a more shocked or concerned variety.

In the middle of the crowd were two larger groups of people, separated only by Melda, Chuck and two others, the statuesque blond he had seen comforting the crying woman earlier today and a man with short dark hair like his own, clad in a red and black check shirt and a pair of denim bootcut jeans.

One side of the cluster was entirely umbral, looking agitated but for the most part, calm. The other side unfortunately were not so placid. Comprised almost entirely of humans, though Vanic could see a few dwarven men and women in their number. This group, as Vanic had previously envisioned, was living out the literal caricature of an angry mob, arms flailing, and shouts being levelled across the hall.

It looked to be the entirely of the umbral collective, numbering thirty-five, facing off against a group about twice that size, with only those few people in the middle trying to maintain the peace as Vanic rushed over to join the peacemakers in the middle.

"Clue me in?" he said as he saw the relief on Melda's face as he approached.

The roar of the crowd was even worse up close, and the discordant screeching of women was centred, unsurprisingly, on the blond in the lycra that he had taken down a peg yesterday.

"Seems like word got out that the missing person is one of us and now everyone has pulled on their prejudice pants," she said as she continued to hold her arms out in front of her like she was mentally willing a huge invisible barrier into existence.

"Wonderful. Just what we needed right now," he said as he ran through crowd control procedures in his head.

A thought then came to him and he turned to look at Rith, who was sat on a bench to the side, taking in the spectacle. He caught his eye and with a grin gave a friendly thumbs up.

"Chuck?" He called out, trying to make himself heard over the crowd.

Chuck, who was currently pushing against the mob, turned at the sound of his name and raised his brows questioningly at Vanic.

"Do me a massive favour and fire off a round into the air please."

Chuck's look of absolute horror told Vanic that this was a man who had never actually had to fire his pistol anywhere outside of a gun range, and he watched as his head swivelled towards Melda, looking for a second opinion.

To her credit, she did seem to consider the idea, if only for a second, before she shrugged.

"Do what he says, Charles."

It was good to see he wasn't the only one casting off the strict protocols and guidelines right now, and that Melda was loosening up in general.

The shot rang out with a loud crack and silenced the whole crowd so fast that there was still time to hear the spent bullet casing hit the ground with a clink.

The absence of sound itself was deafening, like the cacophonous rage of human outburst had just been sucked out of the building. Everyone froze in place and looked to Chuck, who had yet to relax from his stance, both hands raised in the air, firmly clasped around the pistol.

Vanic knew there wouldn't be much time before the shock wore off and that he would have to take control of the situation immediately.

He raised both arms skyward and arced them out like he was directing air traffic as he spoke.

"Can I have everyone's attention please." He shouted with as much authority as he could muster.

The uproar didn't resume. That was a start.

"This ends right now," he bellowed again before lowering his volume slightly. "I think we are all aware there is enough going on here already without you starting fights among yourselves."

"And I suppose you expect us to just sit tight and let these sundowners pick us off one by one?" The lycra clad blond piped in.

He shot her a filthy look before he spoke.

"Firstly, if I hear those words out of your mouth again, you will have made enemies of more than one race of people today."

She grimaced like she just caught scent of something foul she had stepped in.

"Secondly, while it does seem likely that the person responsible is indeed umbral, that hasn't been confirmed and even so…" He paused to put another level of authority back into his voice. "We don't tarnish an entire race by the actions of one person."

He was met with a stone-faced stare from the woman, but more shocking to him was the sensation running through his body at the words he had spoken.

It felt like his entire nervous system was fizzing.

The sheer conviction of his words came as a surprise even to himself. Seeing the level of disgust on this woman's face had made Vanic realise that he in fact unknowingly carried a level of prejudice in himself all these years.

He maintained eye contact with the woman until she eventually looked away and with an exaggerated huff, walked off into the rest of the crowd.

Like with any angry mob, the trick was to take out the ringleader and this situation was no different. As she wandered off to find a place to lick her wounds, the rest of the crowd began to break up like tissue paper in water and slowly dispersed, obviously not wanting their own chance to get chewed out.

Vanic relaxed his posture and felt like he lost a couple of inches in height. He turned to see the mass of black figures also start to separate and was shortly left with his four newly acting deputies.

"That could have gone worse," he said with a smile. "Apologies for your roof."

"If you keep making speeches like that, I think I can allow you a couple more shots at structural damage." Melda tilted her head as she gave him a long inquisitive stare.

CHAPTER TWENTY-FOUR

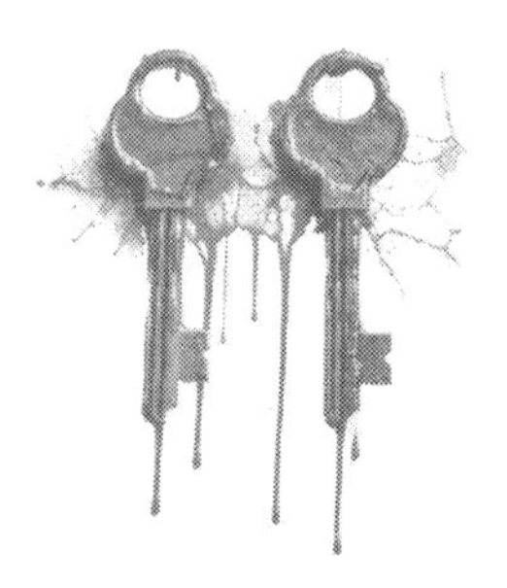

They had swiftly become the last remnants of what could have been a catastrophic situation.

Both crowds had soon dispersed and fallen back into whatever smaller cliques they had formed earlier and the tension in the air was gone, though Vanic could only guess for how long.

He let out a breath, that had been held far longer than he realised and slowly dragged his open palm down across his face.

The man in the checked shirt gave him a weak smile that seemed to say, '*that was tense*' and offered up his hand.

"Karl. Karl Landers," he said as he gave Vanic's hand a firm shake. "That was certainly something, wasn't it?"

He had a low, resonant voice that Vanic often found carried a slight tone of aggression, but here it managed to hold a cadence that was somehow uplifting. He had a strong jaw, deep brown eyes, and a naturally welcoming smile. A stereotypically attractive man with only his aquiline nose, that appeared to have been broken at some point in his life, letting him down.

"You're telling me." Vanic finished taking him in. "Tensions are running high, and people are scared. It's a pressure cooker situation unfortunately. I do have to thank you for stepping in there."

He looked to the others as well now.

"You too, Melda, Chuck, and…?" He looked to the blonde who was still stood with them.

"It's Christine, but everyone calls me Chrissy." She took her turn to shake Vanic's hand.

"Well thank you as well Chrissy. I appreciate you being on hand earlier too with that poor woman. A friend of yours?"

"No," she said, and her face reddened slightly. "It just seemed like the appropriate thing to do in the situation. I'll be honest I rushed over there when I heard the scream, but it seemed like you had things in hand, and I could make better use of my time making sure she was ok." She paused. "Well, as ok as one can be given the circumstances."

"In situations like this, it certainly helps. Chuck, how are you doing?"

Chuck had a vacant expression on his face, and it appeared his mind was somewhere else. He snapped out of it at the sound of his name and turned his attention towards Vanic.

"Huh? Oh. Yeah, I'm doing alright. It felt a bit like one of those scenes from TV." He tried to laugh off his obviously shaken demeanour.

"If the air is all you need to shoot at, I'll consider that a solid win." Vanic patted him on the shoulder.

"Anyway, what about you? How did you get on?" Melda now chimed in.

Vanic looked crestfallen as he replied.

"Nothing. We cleared the whole place and still came up emptyhanded. There's no way anyone is sneaking around me either, given that the others were with me. There's nowhere to hide, but I want to do a full walk-through of all the stores too. Just in case."

"That makes sense," she replied. "Most of them were locked up when the staff left, but there are definitely a few that aren't. It would probably make sense to lock those up as we go too."

"Absolutely. Are you up to doing that with me now? If we get the place more secure before mealtime it at least gives us a little more to tell the crowd. Hopefully that will help keep people calm too."

"Let's be quick about it. I don't like the idea of leaving everyone unsupervised right now."

RITH DECIDED TO COME ALONG FOR THE SEARCH, CITING that on the off chance our killer was hiding out in one the stores, it was best to have greater numbers and to have someone who was armed. Vanic didn't dispute his logic.

Jorhim was asked, but apparently being at the front of the queue for food was a more pressing concern to him, and as he put it - '*You an the elf have got this.*'

It turned out that it didn't matter anyway as it proceeded to be another bust.

Melda was correct in that most of the staff had taken the time to lock up before they had made their way to the commotion of the original scene. The few places that were still unlocked were for the most part, open plan and lacked the ability to hide.

The whole search took hardly anytime, with Melda locking up behind them as they went. Apart from a brief scare in which Rith had leaned on what he thought was a sturdy structure but was in fact a tall stack of shoe boxes, sending it crashing to the ground, causing both Vanic and Melda to panic, it was entirely as devoid of life as Vanic had expected.

They soon found themselves back with the rest of the group, Vanic feeling as frustrated as ever, but at least felt a little better knowing that he'd left no stone unturned.

For tonight's menu, Russel had decided to go for pizza. Another simple option that was easy to throw together, quick to deliver and could cater to both carnivores and vegetarians alike. Plain cheese or pepperoni, those were your choices. Simple.

Vanic sat on the ground with a slice of pepperoni lifted to his mouth, the grease still practically bubbling on the cheese, as he realised he'd somehow managed to form a little clique of his own.

Noah sat in front of him, with his child size cheese pizza on a paper plate. Karl, Chrissy, Russel, Teorre, and a petite girl with a pixie cut, blonde but with an inch of dark hair showing at the roots on the top, sat around them in a small circle.

Jorhim was here too, shovelling what was apparently his third pizza into his mouth, the amount of grease and crumbs that had made a home of his beard was frank-ly impressive. Rith was floating from group to group but kept checking back in at regular intervals.

Chrissy was deep into a rant about the struggles of being a female fitness trainer.

Of course she was.

"What is it you do, Karl?" Vanic asked, trying to move the conversation forward.

"Broadly…" he said, blowing on the slice of pizza he had lifted to his mouth. "I sell furniture."

"And not so broadly?" asked pixie cut.

"I buy old pieces of furniture, refinish them, and sell them on at a profit. It's small, but I have my own store uptown, with a workshop in the back."

"Oh, that's cool, it must be nice being your own boss I suppose," Vanic said as the girl nodded in agreement.

"For sure. So…" Karl said as he danced a mouthful of molten cheese around his mouth. "The more pressing question is, if you've scoured the building and can't find anyone, where are they?"

"That is indeed the question," Vanic replied. "And I don't think just waiting around for them to drop in and say hi, is the best plan of action. Any ideas?"

Teorre, who had somehow decided he was still Noah's babysitter, and so kept close to him since the start, blotted his mouth with a napkin and cleared his throat. "It stands to reason," he said. "That if someone is hiding somewhere you can't find, it must still be somewhere in one of the side corridors. Couldn't we just find some way to barricade them until the police break through the doors?"

"It's not the worst idea, but I'm not sure how well we could actually block them. At best we could provide enough of an obstacle to make it loud for someone trying to leave through the doors."

"Like an early warning system," Karl offered.

"Exactly. But I'm still not convinced that it is where they're hiding. We were thorough in our sweep and it's a mall, there's not exactly anything built in that can serve as some sort of hiding place."

"What's the alternative though?" Chrissy asked. "There's literally nowhere out here that they could be hiding, and they can't have just up and disappeared in broad daylight."

A chill ran down Vanic's spine as his blood froze.

"Fuck." he said as he began getting to his feet in a panic.

"What? What's going on?" Karl asked, sensing the tension that had washed over Vanic.

"Keep an eye on Noah."

Hearing his name, Noah looked up, paying attention for the first time. "Dad? What's happening?" Panic shone from his eyes.

"It's ok, buddy. I just need to go check something." Vanic ruffled the kid's hair.

His brain felt two sizes too big for his skull and the anxiety was washing over him as he dusted the pizza crumbs off his shirt. How could he have been so stupid?

"Van, what is it?" Chrissy asked, the concern noticeable in her voice. The panic was contagious now.

"I'll be right back." He tucked his shirt back into his trousers. "I think I know where he is."

CHAPTER TWENTY-FIVE

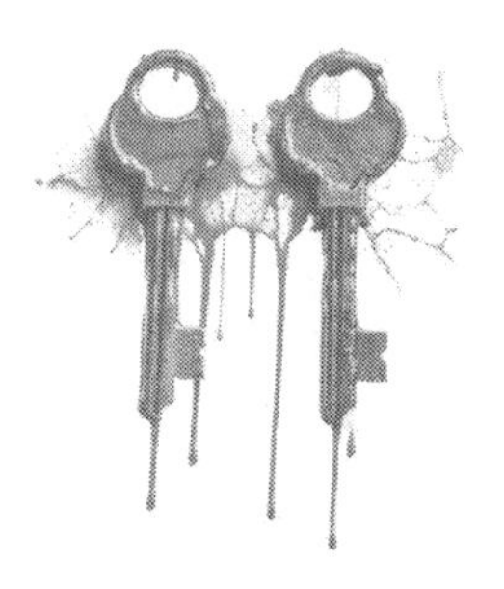

As he began his journey, he struggled to maintain what could only be described as a brisk pace. While the panic was indeed aflame inside him, it would do absolutely nobody any good to see him sprinting through the mall as if demons were at his heels.

Melda of course noticed the sense of urgency on his face from across the hall and gave him a questioning look.

He waved her off and put on his best fake smile before following it up with a light-hearted thumbs up as he carried on towards his destination.

For perhaps the first time, he properly took in his surroundings. The mall itself was so artificial. Clean and white, its many lights managing to illuminate the entire building in its harsh glow. It reminded Vanic of that intense insect's eye of bright lights that a dentist levelled above your head before they came at you with their horrendous implements of torture.

The whole building had a futuristic quality to it. He envisioned all the space stations and ships from sci-fi movies and thought that this would be exactly how it felt to live in a self-contained environment like that. He had never considered how claustrophobic and uncomfortable that would make you feel. They had been trapped here for barely a day and already he was feeling smothered by the synthetic nature of his surroundings. He missed the feel of actual sunlight on his skin, the warm breeze on the air, the very existence of plant life. He genuinely never thought he would be longing to just sit down on the grass and feel the world turn around him.

Had it really been a little over twenty-four hours since this all began?

His head was still aching from the unrelenting headache he had been suffering with and he had a noticeable discomfort in his lower back, presumably from the less-than-ideal sleeping arrangements. He had never gotten round to sourcing any painkillers for his headache and he should probably be making sure to stay hydrated better, but the urgency of the last day hadn't exactly relaxed.

He needed to focus.

Hydration and painkillers were certainly not the top of his list of priorities right now as he carried on towards the corridor that led to Melda's office.

Since putting some distance from the group, he had also quickened his pace some and now the warm sensation of the muscles in his thighs let him know they were there as he walked at an uncomfortable pace, still not allowing himself to burst into a run.

As he made it to the door, he stopped and took a few seconds to compose himself.

He could be wrong.

Part of him hoped he was, and that he wasn't about to find out how stupid he'd been, and things could maintain what was, for now, a slight level of security.

Equal parts of him, the detective parts, wanted to be right. This would bring him the knowledge of where the killer had been hiding, but also open himself up the possibility of hunting them down.

He would have to enlist the help of the others again. In fact, given it would be likely to yield better results, he would be better off gathering a larger group this time round.

He needed to stop getting ahead of himself.

His plan of action could wait until he knew more and had confirmed his hunch. He pushed open the door and stepped into the corridor, readying himself for what might come next.

The corridor felt cooler than it had earlier in the day and the smell of disinfectant in the air seemed to have diminished slightly. The series of spotlights on the ground had vanished too and been replaced with dark circles of shadow from the windows above, confirming it was indeed night-time out in the real world. The basic awareness of the dark, another small detail that had been stripped from him while trapped inside this dome.

The barest hint of his own footsteps was the only sound in the corridor as he slowly stepped forward, making his way towards the nearest door on his left. A part of him knew what he would find before he got there, and he held his contained breath as he slowly turned the tubular metal handle and opened the door.

The lockers lining the back wall all appeared as earlier to be untouched, but as he looked towards the right side of the room his suspicions were confirmed.

The clothing that had been left spread across the table and chair were gone.

Fuck.

A shiver ran down his spine and his whole body felt like it was covered in spiders, a full body itch of discomfort.

He grabbed the chair and launched it across room where it collided with both the far wall and the end lockers, delivering a loud metallic clang before falling to the floor, two of its legs bent wildly out of the shape and a large crack running down the back of the seat.

In hindsight it seemed so obvious, and he was furious with himself for not putting the pieces together sooner.

The killer had sneaked away from the group, ambushed and killed the man, before stringing him up in his sick theatrical display. He had then made his way across the hall and into this room before stripping off his clothes and stepping out into one of the beams of sunlight in the corridor.

Essentially taking himself off the board for the entire day and leaving them chasing ghosts.

He felt so stupid. It seemed obvious now that he thought about it. He knew they were searching for an umbral, why hadn't be put the pieces together sooner?

Stop.

It was pointless to stand here beating himself up about what he didn't do, when making plans for what to do next was of a far greater concern.

He needed to get back to the group.

His own incompetence aside, the most important update that came from this was the knowledge that, with the sunlight gone, the killer was now skulking around in the building with nowhere to hide.

Caution could be thrown to the wind right now and he darted out of the room and back down the corridor. He needed to get back to the others as fast as he could and get a group together to start another search.

Opening the door out into the main hall, he began to sprint back towards the crowd, his thighs burning as he ran.

It was then that the lights went out.

CHAPTER TWENTY-SIX

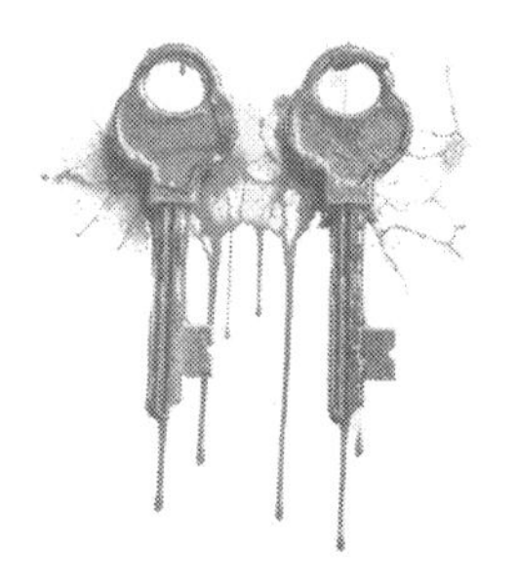

The instantaneous transition from relative silence to that communal scream right as a rollercoaster drops, was harrowing. Even more so given that they were surrounded in abject darkness.

After a moment of frozen terror stopped him in his tracks, he continued his course in the direction he assumed was correct, not faltering in his pace.

The sounds of the commotion were enough to aim for, but after a few seconds small pockets of light began to appear in a cluster up ahead, like fireflies coasting the edges of a lake on a cool autumn evening.

The people with the foresight to switch off their phones earlier had begun to pull them out and switch on their torches, small beams of light pinging into existence but not providing much more than a couple of metres reprieve from the dark.

He hit the centre of the group about the same time as the outlying members of the crowd, drawing in on themselves like a great black hole, panic causing everyone to fall into the most basic primal instincts of safety in numbers.

Up close the various pockets of torchlight were enough to take in the immediate crowd, and Vanic was pleased to see that even in their panic, the children had all been corralled into the centre of the group, Noah, to his relief, firmly in the centre. Chuck and Melda were also in the middle of the cluster, and he was pleased to see that they had clearly factored in both protecting the children but also placing their sole pistol in an area with at least a modicum of visibility.

Even though instinct had done most of the work here already, people were still in full panic mode and the screams and cries of many were a din that wasn't exactly helping. Part of the group were either made of stronger stuff or just in a state of shock, as their silent faces seemed to be carrying more vacuous expressions.

Vanic went first to Noah, leaning down and wrapping an arm around his shoulders to give him a squeeze, followed by a wink as he saw him smile up at him. The kid was fearless. He then moved to Melda and Chuck.

"Funny story." He turned to look at him. "I was on my way back to let you know that I'd found where they were hiding and that they now had no place to hide. Guess I was about to speak too soon."

"I don't think we've got the same definition of funny," Chuck said.

Vanic could see the beads of sweat running down the side of Chucks face, highlighted by the sparse beams of light in their vicinity.

"I don't think I'm known for my rapier wit; it is true. We need to get these lights back on pronto though. These phones aren't going to hold out for long."

As they began to brainstorm what the best plan of action would be for getting to the nearest control panel in hopes of getting the lights back on, the crowd around them began to shift. The cries of panic seemed to subside as previously hysterical people stopped to take in what was happening around them.

Though it was difficult to see, especially with the limited glow coming from various phones, Vanic could make out the shapes of dozens of people starting to push their way to the borders of the group.

It was the umbral populace of the crowd. All of them.

They were moving to the outside of the huddled crowd and forming a large circle around it, each standing a couple of metres apart from each other, their backs to the group.

"What are they doing?" Vanic asked Melda, who appeared to be one of the only members of their shadowy contingent not taking up a place in their circle.

"Isn't it obvious? They're forming a protective wall."

"I don't understand.," he said confused. "Why?"

"Look, you just said yourself that these phones aren't going to last long, and it's your only means of seeing who's coming. Well, we are more than capable of seeing in the dark. If anyone is going to try to rush the group, they'll see them coming."

For the second time today Vanic was gobsmacked.

This group, who had only hours ago been on the receiving end of an angry mob's rage, were stepping up to protect those very same people. He was starting to realise just how small minded he had been for such a long time.

This wasn't the time to ponder his personal outlook and accidental bigotry though. They needed to make full use of the situation right away.

Once again though, as Vanic was about to start formulating a slightly better plan, they were interrupted.

Off in the distance at the far end of the mall, near one of the doors leading to the staff corridors, a bright light burst into life, casting an ominous red glow across the building.

Though it was a fair distance away, there was a noticeable hissing sound emanating from it as the source of the light washed over the area.

"What now?" questioned Melda, wishing to break the silence.

Vanic gritted his teeth, the sequence of events was again playing out in such a mocking manner.

"That's an invitation if ever I saw one. A literal flare in the dark, pretty dramatic."

The irony of it was not lost on him. The flare being a means of signalling for help, and yet this beacon of red light was inviting only danger.

Melda looked at him with an alarming amount of concern on her face. "You're not thinking of going, are you? It's clearly a trap."

He took a moment to scan the area as well as he could, given their current luminosity concerns, and looked around at the array of worried faces he could make out.

He felt his stomach knot as the dread of what he had to do took hold. He thought of Noah, the single greatest achievement in his life, and of Sarah left waiting in a terrifying state of limbo. Waves of regret began to wash over him for even being here. He thought of Roma, and the regret he felt for choosing not to call her when he could. It didn't matter what the stakes were now, he knew what he had to do.

"Of course it is. It's taunting, and we know it's clearly aimed at me. I don't doubt it's a trap, but I also don't see what other options we have. If I don't go, things aren't going to just stop. Bottom line, it's my job to do so."

She didn't look convinced.

"Part of me thinks they won't expect me to just walk in there though, and so maybe that's the best thing I can do. My priority here is keeping people safe and if it means casually walking into the lion's den, then so be it. While I'm doing that though, it's buying more time out here. I'm going to need you to take a few people and get these fucking lights back on."

She just nodded as she listened to his plan.

"Take a couple of volunteers, ideally armed or with phones still capable of lighting the way, and get this place lit up. Don't take any risks. The slightest sign of something seeming off, I want you back here with the group, but if we can use this time to light things back up its going to help everyone, myself included."

"I can do that." She moved to walk away.

Vanic grabbed her by the arm.

"I just wanted to say I'm incredibly thankful for all your help. No, don't shrug it off, I really mean it. You have been a rock for everyone here and I don't think this place would be as held together if it wasn't for you."

Melda looked more shocked right now than he had seen her this whole time.

"I'm serious. I don't know how well you're appreciated here, but once we're out of here, I'd like to put in some serious words of praise to your employers."

He let her go and took a few steps towards the glow before he stopped and turned.

"Chuck." he called out. "Stay vigilant and don't let those kids out of your sight."

Chuck already had his pistol drawn but it was resting casually at his side and after a puzzled couple of seconds, his face hardened slightly into a no-nonsense resolve, and he gave Vanic a nod.

With That, Vanic set his sights on the slightly diminishing crimson glow from across the mall and began his walk into what he knew would be trouble.

CHAPTER TWENTY-SEVEN

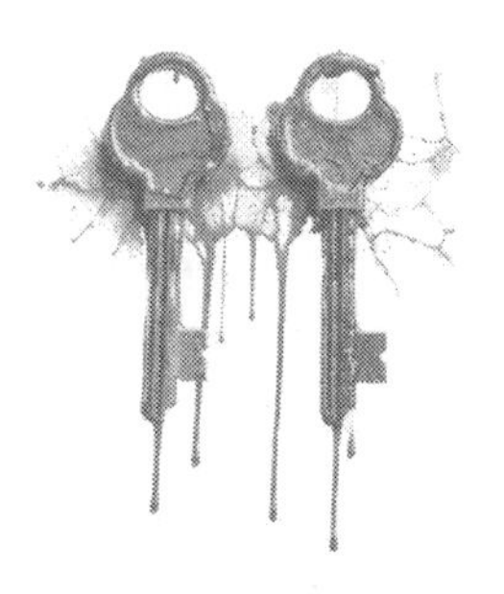

Reaching the door at the end of the mall, Vanic saw the flare laying on the ground. The floor beneath it was charred and coated in a black sooty residue.

He cautiously picked it up and held it out in front of him as he did a full three-sixty taking in the immediate vicinity, the flare casting its crimson hue out into the darkness as he spun.

Nothing.

He wasn't surprised. It was clear that whoever this was, they were leading him in an obvious direction. He knew that stepping through the door was about to start him on a path that would quickly be out of his control, but he also knew that he didn't have much choice.

He swapped the flare to his left hand and bracing himself, pushed open the door into the corridor before tentatively stepping in.

Inside the confines of the corridor, the sulphur stink of the flare in his outstretched hand was the prevalent odour filling his nostrils and though the intensity of it was beginning to ebb, it still managed to cast enough red light to illuminate his way. Its diminished output added an element of illusion to the walkway, making the lengthy corridor appear even longer than it was.

Having already made a couple of passes through the whole building in the last twenty-four hours, it came as no surprise to Vanic that the killer had chosen the most labyrinthine of the private areas to serve as his gauntlet.

He felt the fear of moving forward, working hard against the rage and anger that was building inside him, a scale teetering up and down as his emotions fought.

Before he reached the first door on his journey, he stopped to consider whether it was worth switching to his phone as a source of light instead. Considering the electronic dead-zone the mall had become, he had only used it to periodically check the time. In fact, the last time he'd used it properly was to take pictures of Noah and the animals at the zoo. Something that now seemed like forever ago.

Pulling the phone from his pocket, he saw that it still had thirteen percent battery life, surely enough to last a while using its torch, and clicked on the light, sending a modest beam of yellow out in front of him.

Reaching the door to his left, he aimed his phone into the small round window and tilted it left and right to take in the room, a complete recreation of the staffroom on the other side of building, with nothing but lockers, table, and chairs.

He soon realised the biggest problem with using his phone for light was that it was directional and did little to illuminate anything else around him. The flare at least cast its glow across the surrounding area.

Pocketing the phone, he decided to instead carry on along the corridor with the flare.

Working his way slowly down the hall as it took multiple turns was a tense and unsettling situation, made entirely worse by the red on black hellscape he was forced to endure as his only source of light. The ominous setting reminded Vanic of many of the horror movies he had watched in his teen years and part of him was expecting to hear sinister children's laughter or the eerie tintinnabulation of chimes.

A cold shiver ran down his spine.

Cautiously continuing along, he stopped at each door on the way to check rooms he expected to be empty but didn't want to leave himself open to some hidden ambush before he eventually came to a junction. To his left the corridor trailed off and led to a set of stairs leading up to the next level. To his right, it carried on a small way before eventually stopping at a large set of steel double doors.

His stomach convulsed and a wave of dread and sickness washed over him as he realised where he had ended up.

The intimidating doors ahead of him led to the warehouse and loading bay. An expansive space filled with aisles of shelves, stacked pallets, and a multitude of places to hide in the dark.

The hiss of the flare was now barely a crackle and the light it cast was dwindling further, bringing the glow tighter around him as he pressed a tentative hand on the door and pushed it open as he stepped through.

CHAPTER TWENTY-EIGHT

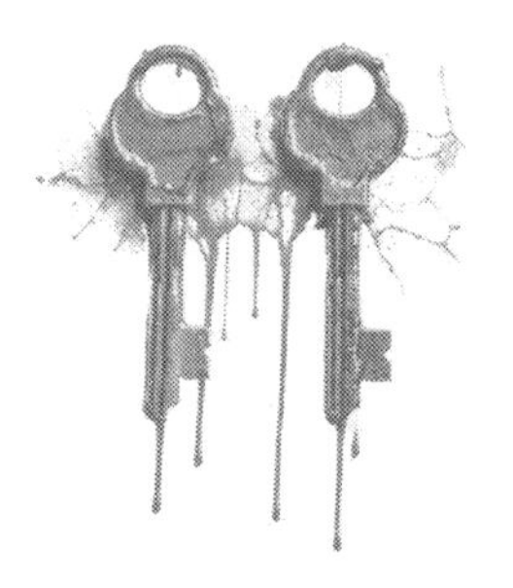

Stepping into the warehouse, the temperature immediately dropped a few degrees and there was an overpowering damp odour in the air, like sawdust and cardboard boxes soaked in rainwater. Somehow mingling the dry smell of recycled paper with an acrid mildewy stench.

Rows upon rows of red metal bracketed shelves ran parallel along both sides of the warehouse. Huge square pallets were scattered throughout the middle of the room in no discernible pattern, stacked high with a variety of boxes or unusual shapes wrapped up tightly in plastic.

Two school-bus-yellow forklift trucks were butted up against the far-left wall, alongside half a dozen smaller pallet trucks in a mixture of yellows and orange. The right wall housed a mixture of steel ladders and larger warehouse ladders on wheels, painted a cobalt blue.

At the back wall like the eyes of the room, were two huge metallic shutters that opened out onto the side of the mall for trucks to back into for unloading. Sandwiched between both shutters was a raised platform that Vanic assumed served as an ideal vantage point for supervisors to oversee the unloading of goods.

Stood at the centre of this elevation was a dark figure, hard to make out at this distance with the darkness shrouding them like a blanket of midnight. Even from this distance the figure looked poised and waiting.

Vanic swallowed and slowly stepped forward into the room, holding the flare aloft ahead of him as he inched towards the figure, every muscle in his body feeling taut and ready.

As he began to close the gap, the figure took a couple of steps forward and Vanic could make out the silhouette of the figure a little better. He looked to hold himself in a strong, confident manner and Vanic could see he was slowly flexing and relaxing his right hand at his side, the claw-like talons angular and sharp looking as the fingers relaxed.

"Detective Vanic Bradley, face to face at last." The figure spoke out, a gravelly undertone carrying through the raspy voice, which had a relaxed, well-spoken quality to it.

"I was beginning to think you might decline my invitation, but no, we both know what kind of man you are."

The voice had an air of familiarity to it that Vanic couldn't place, but it still managed to send a shiver down his spine.

"That seems like an awfully loaded statement coming from a man with so much blood on his hands." Vanic dropped his pace to mere baby steps as he inched forward, holding the dying flare up high. He was shocked at how calm and level his voice was, despite the situation.

"Perhaps." He retained the same posture, showing no signs of moving. "I suppose you would be quite the authority on the volume of blood one might have on their hands, no? Or does it not count for my kind? We don't bleed as such I suppose." He put a lot of emphasis on the word '*bleed*', dragging it out for emphasis.

"Is that what this is about?" Vanic spat, fear being slowly overtaken by anger now. "Did I take down someone you know, and this is some pathetic vendetta? Because let me tell you, anyone I've dealt with has been a criminal and had only themselves to blame. And this..." he bellowed. "You've murdered four innocent people to get my attention. That's worse than anything I've done."

"Now, now, Van. There's no reason to get angry. Try to keep that temper of yours in check if you wouldn't mind."

Vanic guessed there was still a thirty-to-forty-meter separation of space between them and knew that rushing him wasn't really an option just yet as he continued to slowly advance.

"My temper? You're a killer on the loose in a sealed building. I think my anger is pretty fucking justified."

"Indeed. We do find ourselves cut off from the rest of the city, don't we?" He raised his arms skyward, gesturing at their expanse. "A predicament afforded to us by this very city's prejudices. It's interesting, no? That there just happened to be a failsafe that would cut off the entire umbral community from leaving. Keeping us all locked away nice and safe in the bubbles your kind have built for us."

"I'm sure there was a good reason for it to be in place."

"A platitude I'm sure they shared with all the other animals in cages." His tone was mocking now. "How was the zoo by the way? Young Noah enjoyed himself, I hope."

Vanic's blood boiled, and he reflexively took a few quick steps forward before pushing that building rage back down again and slowing his step.

"I'm through with this bullshit. I'm sure this makes you feel like a big man, but it ends here. I'm taking you in."

"Oh, the conviction. My heart is all a flutter. Do tell me how you plan to do that exactly?"

Vanic moved his outstretched arm to the left, brandishing the flare a little higher as he reached about to the back of his waistband with the other.

He brought it back around swiftly and levelled the pistol up at his target, who still stood calmly on the elevated platform.

"The same way I take down everybody else," he said with determination in his voice.

"My, my, and how do you expect to do that with an unloaded gun?"

a blast went off like the punctuation of his statement, a loud pop quickly followed by a clatter of metal.

The shot went intentionally wide, hitting the corrugated metal shutter on the left. The man, to his credit, didn't falter.

"Well." There was a pause that felt as though it stretched on for an eternity. "I hope you haven't taken the only loaded gun and left the crowd unprotected, Van."

The standard issue Glock 19 has a 15-round magazine. After securing one of the empty pistols left as a distasteful taunt at the last murder site, Vanic had taken Chuck to one side and acquired some of his rounds for himself. Taking ten of the 9mm rounds and leaving Chuck with five. Four currently.

"They're still plenty protected from you, don't worry," he said as he continued moving forward, adopting a new stance as he carefully crossed his feet in front of each other as he walked.

"Who said anything about me" he replied, his tone now dripping with sly sarcasm.

The lighting suddenly bloomed back into life with a chain of clicks that echoed through the room, and a monotonous hum that had previously gone unnoticed droned in the background.

He had bought enough time for Melda to get the power back on, that was a good sign at least. The levelled playing field of vision was also something he was thankful for.

For the first time, he was finally face to face with the killer. A man of noticeable stature, with a plain white button-down shirt, the sleeves rolled up to the elbows, and simple black trousers. The delicate tendrils of ink on his head were running back over the top of his skull, like an overly preened and gelled hairstyle. He was barefoot, the ends of the toes coming to similar points as the fingertips.

This was not the man from the raid. A fact that momentarily send his mind reeling and he had to focus hard to push down the panic that was trying to burst free. He needed to stay calm right now.

"What?" he replied. His senses were now on full alert, and for a second, he was sure he heard movement behind him and moved to turn.

"I said, who said protection from me?" Again, there was a solid emphasis on 'me'. As if following up with an attack he added "And I think it's Noah you should be worried about."

The air left Vanic's lungs as he seethed and while it was clear he was doing all he could to push his buttons, it was working. The anger of having a direct threat to his son was immense, but it battled hard with the fear and dread that was also levelled with the threat.

He dropped the now unnecessary flare and held the pistol firmly in both hands, levelled at the man's chest.

"Is that so?" Vanic croaked.

"Certainly so. Not protection from me. And it would seem, not Zavrin either."

The impact caught Vanic square in the back of the head, leaving him no time to respond. The gun in his hands went off as he fell, feeling only the jarring pain shoot up through his body as his knees hit the floor, before losing consciousness.

CHAPTER TWENTY-NINE

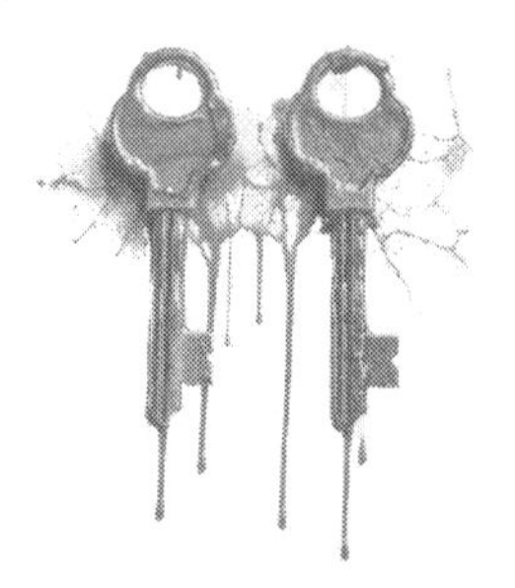

At fourteen, Vanic had gone through a noticeable growth spurt. This shooting up in height hadn't made a difference to his obvious babyface and he had yet to fill out his new proportions, which left him relatively tall but still gangly.

His mother had told him, light heartedly, that the biggest change he had gone through was in his smell. According to her, he now stank like a teenage boy. She joked that it would be a massive relief to her nasal receptors when he finally started to notice girls. She also made a comment about how it would give him a different reason to take long showers, but he didn't quite understand what she meant by that.

Gym class had not long finished up and he currently understood what she meant by the smell. The whole gym was thick with the musk of teenage boys.

Today's class had been dodgeball, a sport that to him, felt less about the game and more about forcing kids to exercise using the medium of fear - keep running or take a large red ball to the face.

Vanic had been chosen to stay behind at the end of the lesson to gather up all the aforementioned spongey balls of pain. It was alarming to him how many of them were often found with wet patches of presumably some kids spittle on them.

He was busy gathering up the balls into the first of the three net sacks, trying his best to round them up quickly so he could get back to the locker room and get changed, that he didn't notice the other boys that had crept back into the hall.

A ball caught him directly on the side of the face with a loud slap and the shock made him jump. The following throb in his ear was instantaneous and he grimaced, turning as he heard vicious laughter.

"Sorry, Van. Thought it might help you gather them up faster that way."

The three boys that had made Vanic's life hell, all obsidian and filled with menace approached him.

Like his day wasn't already going terribly.

"Not now, ok? I just want to get this done," he said feebly, knowing full well it wasn't going to make a difference.

"Did you both hear that? Karn, Zavrin, it appears Vanic doesn't appreciate your help."

"Very ungrateful," Karn said in mock hurt as the long tendrils of shadow that fell from his head seemed to ripple across his shoulders.

His face soured and he stepped forward, red ball clutched tightly in both hands. 'We're just trying to help,' he said as he shoved the ball hard into Vanic's chest, forcing him backwards and slamming him into the wooden wall bar apparatus that lined the walls of the gym.

It shook as he bounced off it and Vanic used the momentum to shove Karn hard in the chest with both hands, though it barely moved him. "Just leave me alone!"

The boy's face hardened further, and a sneer grew across his face like a gash carved into the very darkness.

He returned the shove, both hands pummelling into Vanic's chest, again bouncing him off the wall bars. The pain registered across his back this time and panic started to set in.

Realising the futility of trying to fight, *it was three on one after all,* he tried to force his way past Karn with a shoulder barge to no avail.

The boy was stronger than him and on blocking his escape, immediately shoved him back again into the shaking apparatus before stepping in even further to close off any escape route.

The other two stood in silence, fixated on the show, and massive grins cut across their evil faces.

"It's no use trying to run out on us, runt. You've still got all these balls to collect," Karn said as he kicked the sack Vanic had dropped, causing the collected balls to begin rolling out across the ground.

Accepting his fate, Vanic decided he wasn't going to go down without a fight and seized the opportunity of Karn drawing close to put all his strength into a headbutt.

The pain was immediate as Vanic's forehead collided with the bridge of his attacker's nose with a loud crunch. It hurt like hell, but he imagined it to be far worse to be on the receiving end.

Karn let out a low roar, guttural and filled with rage before he lunged forward grabbing Vanic round the throat with both hands so tightly that he could feel the sharp tips of his fingers cutting into the back of his neck and began to repeatedly bounce him off the wall bars as he throttled him.

Vanic's vision began to cloud as he was choked and the painful impacts on his back were barely registering anymore.

The wall bars on the other hand, were not weathering the abuse so well and each slam seemed to shake the bars even further.

He felt as though his consciousness was about to fail him when something dropped down from above.

One of the large medicine balls that were stored on the top of the apparatus had fallen with the impact and he watched as it now plummeted down and collided with Karn's head.

There were the combined sounds of a solid thud, like someone hitting a punching bag, twinned with a sickening crack as Karn's head tilted to an anatomy defying angle seconds before he dropped to the floor.

Like every teenage boy, Vanic assumed he was indestructible and the idea of a falling ball, even one with the weight of a medicine ball, doing any serious damage seemed completely implausible. He also knew that the umbral people were naturally built much tougher than the other races and so it seemed even less of a possibility.

None of these thoughts did much to remove the vision of Karn Lying before him on the ground, motionless with his head cocked unnaturally to the side, his inky hair tendrils splayed out above him.

His two companions were stood aghast, with nothing but horror on their faces and silence on their lips.

Vanic did the only thing he could do in that moment.

He screamed.

CHAPTER THIRTY

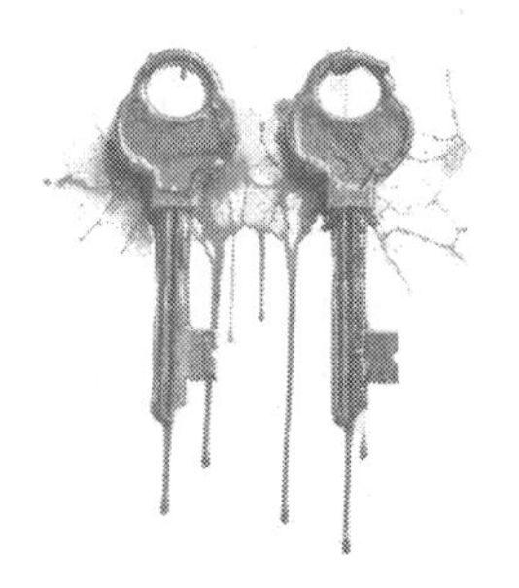

The overhead fluorescent lights blinded him. It was like staring directly into the sun as Vanic tried opening his eyes, blinking the painful white glow away. Blurry dark silhouettes hovered in front of him as he tried to focus his vision.

The pain in his temples paired with the blow he had taken to the back of his head, encircling his entire skull like a crown of agony. His mouth was thick with saliva and tasted metallic and sharp.

The shapes weaving in front of him began to take more cohesive forms and he worryingly remembered where he was.

"Looks like he's back with us," said the first blur, straightening up from its bowed form in front of him.

Blur number two took a few steps forward, closing the gap between them, its head cocking in a sympathetic manner.

Looking around as things started to appear a little crisper and more focused, Vanic could see his feet splayed out before him and for the first time was aware of the rigid plastic feel at his back.

He had been moved.

Given the view ahead of him, presumably he'd been propped up against one of the stacked pallets in the warehouse. The two figures before him had piled up more behind them and to his left, the red metal shelving units arched out, forming long narrow pathways between them.

"Welcome back to the land of the living, Van," said the second figure, now that Vanic's vision had now cleared enough to register as the man he had only recently been looking at down the barrel of his gun.

Vanic clenched his eyes shut and let out a short, exaggerated moan that was the love of child of both sigh and groan. "I don't remember accepting you into a first name basis."

The man steepled his fingers and smiled in glee. "There he is. That's the man I've been expecting."

He began to pace left and right before him. His partner stepping back, leaning against a pallet seemingly leaving him the spotlight.

"For years," he continued. "I considered that maybe it really was just a terrible accident. Perhaps you had no hand in it at all. An unfortunate course of events just played out rather unfavourably. A tragedy if you will"

The voice again seemed familiar to Vanic, but he was still struggling to place it.

"Oh, I dwelled on it of course. I mean, who can really say they wouldn't take the loss of a best friend badly after all? But once all that rage subsided and some time had passed, I thought, Othum, accidents happen. Your friend was taken away from you and there's really nobody to blame but the fates."

Othum.

The name landed like a bullet to the chest and Vanic felt his heartrate double. He felt like he was baking under a thousand spotlights, beads of sweat starting to trickle down his face.

"But then," his tone shifted, taking on a more malevolent quality. "I happened to catch a wonderful piece of news footage. An attack on City Hall, halted by the wonderful Dalton police department, and who did I see? Detective Vanic Bradley. Enforcer of the law. A no-nonsense cop, coming down hard on the criminal underbelly…"

Vanic cut him off, steadying himself with his right palm on the ground and moved to stand up. "Are you just here to read me my resume, or is there a point coming?"

Lightning fast, Othum shot forward and connected a kick into Vanic's stomach, knocking the wind out of him and dropping him back to the ground.

"Coming down hardest it would seem, on the umbral community," he continued as he stepped back again. "Quite the name you've built for yourself. Spoken in hushed tones by all. And then I find out that you even have your own little moniker."

He spat on the floor for effect and Vanic couldn't help but notice that even this looked to have an inky quality to it.

"The Lamplighter. How very clever. The scourge of darkness indeed."

He made no further attempt to stand, but locked eyes with this raving psychopath. "A name you'll find was given to me by the low lives in the city. I had nothing to do with it." Vanic snapped in response, though he momentarily felt a newfound level of shame burning inside him.

"Yes, I'm sure. But anyway, this got me thinking. Thinking that this all sounds absolutely typical of a man that hates our kind. A man that would certainly orchestrate the accidental death of a boy he hated." He accents the word accidental with quotations marks using his fingers, their claw like ends working to full effect.

Vanic lost any attempt at keeping him cool, and raised himself up again as he shouted back – "That's what this is about? You tortured me for years and didn't stop until your own brutality saw one of you off. I'm not glad it happened, but it did. And now you come here decades later and start killing innocent people to get my fucking attention?"

His outburst was met with nothing but a cold hard stare, and the self-righteous sneer now gone from Othum's face.

"It's pathetic." He tried to stand again, forcing himself off the ground with his hands. "And if you're quite finished monologuing, can we just get on with whatever the fuck this is?"

He raised himself up to full height and leaned back on the misshapen plastic wrapped pallet behind him and drew in a painful breath, taking in the look of disgust that had now affixed itself to both faces before him. "Because I'd rather die right here than have to listen to another word of your pitiful pissbaby diatribe."

The pain in his head was still pulsing consistently and now paired with the dull ache in his stomach from the kick he received to merge the throbbing in his temples with a feeling of nausea.

For a few seconds, Vanic's eyes locked onto both aggressors, their distaste for his words causing a vicious snarl from each of them. His outburst had obviously hit a nerve, and for a moment if felt like three young boys, facing off in the school cafeteria, before they quickly composed themselves and he soon found himself staring at their self-important sneers once more.

His eyes began darting about the room, searching for something that could be used as a weapon. Anything that could be used to defend himself and balance the odds. His gun was nowhere to be seen and he assumed they had already taken it off the board.

"Are you really so keen to die, Van?" Othum broke the awkward silence of the standoff. "This isn't all about you, not really."

"It feels an awful lot like it's about me."

"A revolution must start somewhere I suppose. It felt like the most poignant way to kick things off. To rid the world of someone so frankly abhorrent." He took a few steps back and leaned on the pallet behind him, mirroring Vanic's position.

Vanic let out a short burst of laughter and reached up to rub the back of his head, looking at the small amount of thick blood on his fingers as he brought the hand back down.

"Just because you buy into this narrative doesn't make it true. Karn's death was his own fault, and I haven't done anything since then that wasn't justified within the eyes of the law."

"Lies!" Othum shouted, once again losing his cool. "You have seeded yourself into a system designed by your people to keep your filthy boots on our throats. Gathering us all into wonderfully manageable bubbles to keep us in line. There was a time when we were free to do as we pleased, not governed by this forced captivity you parade as inclusion and progress."

"This is where I'm getting confused. The whole reason for the domed communities, much like this mall, was to give your kind the freedom to exist during the day. How have you managed to spin that into an attack?"

"It doesn't matter how large a cage you give an animal, it's still in a cage," Othum said as a grin split his face, revealing the jagged onyx teeth inside.

"And nobody is forcing you to stay there. They exist to provide a place to live during the day. If you don't want that, then don't live there. Don't stand here spewing some twisted narrative about control. You're manipulating the facts to suit your own agenda, a frankly insane and dangerous one."

"Am I?" he hissed, his voice like nails down a chalkboard. "Or could it be that everyone has been conditioned to believe that this is all a work of progress and are too naïve to see the truth?"

"Oh please." Vanic said as he rolled his eyes. "You know what's right and everyone else is just too dumb to know the truth. Is that really the angle you're going for? Let me tell you about men who think they know what people want, something I've dealt with many times in my career. They're narcissistic monsters. The kind of people that think no means yes, and that the other person just isn't enlightened enough to make their own decisions. Well let me tell you, no man has ever climbed off a crying woman and thought she was convinced."

Othum's face visibly soured at this, but Vanic wasn't done.

"Yet here you are, murdering innocent people because you think the roof over your head is what? Some sort of cage? Nobody is clipping your wings here."

Othum began to clap his hands mockingly. "Bravo. No really, that was quite the speech, don't you think Zavrin? Very enthusiastic. I'd have said you should run for office if you weren't soon to be shuffling off this mortal coil."

The pain in Vanic's stomach was beginning to pass, and though the same couldn't be said about his head, Vanic was feeling steadier on his feet now. He had moved past shock and into rage and was now becoming aware that he was dealing with a dangerous and delusional madman. His mind flicked the switch into work mode, and he evaluated the situation quickly in his head.

As the situation currently stood, he was now facing not one, but two perpetrators of this whole affair, a veritable bloodbath centred around him. The way Othum was talking, or, in this instance raving, this was just the start of some grander scheme and Vanic was just the precursor. His mind was reeling at the whole situation. The teenage bully all grown up to become a calculating, remorseless murderer.

He needed to try and end this now. He thought of Noah, and all the other people that were counting on him. Countless people locked inside this building, just wanting to go home and be with their families. He couldn't fail them now.

There was no telling what their plan was beyond this insular revenge plot, and there was a whole building full of collateral damage to think about, including his own son. Unarmed and outnumbered, the odds were weighed heavily in their favour. Even one-on-one the odds weren't great, the hardiness of the umbral people was well documented, and the advantage of natural sharp claws that could rend flesh with ease only added to that problem.

"You've needlessly slaughtered four people in cold blood just to get me here." Vanic began to scan the room again. He needed to buy some time to figure out a plan of action. "It seems you've been tracking me for some time, why not just pick me off on my own? It sounds like you'd have had plenty of opportunities to do so."

"True, but it would lack a certain sense of style. Something like this needed to be given a level of grandeur worthy of the opponent."

He could run. He didn't fancy his chances of outrunning them both, but there was a tactical advantage to numbers if he could make it back to the group, and it wasn't like they could escape from here. If he could make It back to everyone, they could easily barricade both doors from this section and hold them there until the reinforcements outside broke through.

"Is that all this is to you? Some kind of game? Killing people just to make a big show of how smart you are. Well, where do we go from here?"

"It's really quite simple." Othum pushed his sleeves further up his forearms. "You and I, we fight to the death. Just like our ancestors who drew proper lines in the sand and didn't allow this pretence of living in harmony together."

Running wasn't going to be an option then.

Vanic clenched his fists and set his feet, grounding himself as he felt every muscle in his body tense. If he was to die today, he would give as good as he got. Keeping his eyes locked firmly on Othum, the tension in the air was palpable and they had reached a point where things could erupt into chaos at any moment.

The uncomfortable silence was shattered by the sudden crashing open of the heavy doors from the warehouse, quickly followed by a high whirring sound that whistled past Vanic's shoulder.

A short *thunk* sound like an axe splitting wood filled the air as the arrow found its mark, burying deep into the shoulder of Zavrin, sending him spiralling to the ground.

Vanic didn't dare waste even a second of this opening to turn and register the location of the attack. Maintaining his focus on Othum, who was facing the direction of this intrusion, suddenly wide-eyed with horror, he darted forward and barrelled into him, mustering all his energy into a tackle that sent them both crashing through the pallet behind him.

CHAPTER THIRTY-ONE

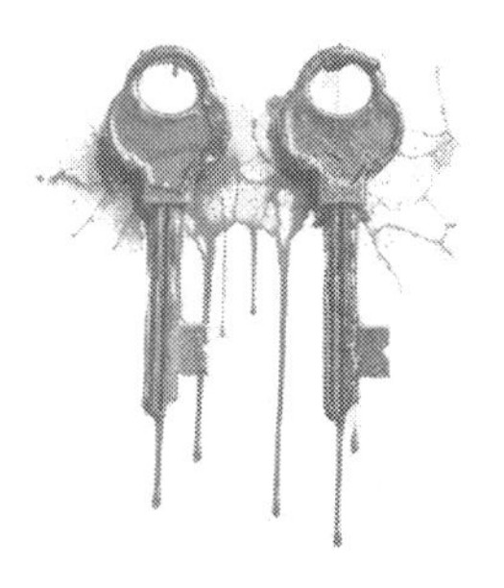

Melda stood at the centre of the crowd with Chuck and Chrissy, surveying the area and doing her best to retain what little composure she could. Right up until the lights had gone out, she'd been running on auto-pilot, doing what needed to be done and hadn't stopped to really consider the danger. It dawned on her now that she had been in the presence of four very dead and mutilated bodies and her reaction was to jump straight to - *what do we do now?*

The biggest surprise for her was how exhilarating this situation was. As terrifying as this all was, it had given her a strange sense of purpose. Working alongside detective Bradley had been oddly fulfilling and, though it both embarrassed and saddened her, she'd received more positive praise in the past twenty-four hours than she had in years of her career.

After an unhindered and successful journey to get the lights back on, accompanied by a more than willing group of protectors, they had swiftly returned to the group.

Though proper vision had now been restored none of the crowd looked any less tense or uneasy, choosing to still gather in a relative cluster of bodies. The continuous jerking of heads on high alert was very apparent and it didn't look like anyone was ready to relax just yet.

As they made their way back to the centre of the crowd, it was soon revealed that a member of their umbral collective had headed off in the direction of detective Bradley. Information that for a few of their number had sparked an instant decision to follow suit. The elven man in the group had rationalised that if a would-be hero had run off to help Vanic, strength in numbers could only be bolstered by their doing so too. He then put a dampener on that idea by pointing out that in contrast, if the disappearing person in question wasn't so altruistic, and that perhaps there were more wolves hidden in the fold, then their help might be even more appreciated.

The elf, along with the surly dwarf who wouldn't stopping swinging that damned bat, and Karl, her saviour from the earlier crowd hysteria, had headed off soon after. The statuesque blonde had wanted to go too, but Karl managed to convince her that it was likely best, as he put it, not to put all their eggs in one basket and so she had stuck around.

Melda had to admit, she felt like she should be doing something more.

While it was obvious that there were a lot of scared people here and tension and anxiety were permeating through their group like an airborne pathogen being gradually sucked up by their number, it was also clear that the adrenaline was high in some of the party, and it felt like standing around wasn't the best use of their time.

People were visibly tense and seemed like they were waiting for imminent disaster. A small number of women were still openly weeping in crumpled heaps on the ground, friends or loved ones doing their best to calm them. The parents at the centre of the crowd were doing their best to remain stoic in the face of fear for the kids' sake, though anyone else could see these masks were starting to slip. The children too were becoming bored and restless, their true understanding of the situation may have been lacking, but they were getting antsy.

The blonde still looked as disgruntled as ever as she spoke with Chuck at her side, ranting about the fact that if she wasn't a woman the others wouldn't have suggested she stay behind. Chuck was doing his best to calm her, though his best happened to come in the form of just silently nodding along to her tirade and carelessly scratching at the side of his head with the barrel of his gun.

Melda hoped that whatever trouble Vanic had rushed off into, was something he could handle. She hated to admit it, but she'd found herself warming to him almost immediately, his serious manner being cast off at times when he let his personality shine through. His outburst during the mass stand-off earlier had equally surprised her, and she'd began to wonder if she'd had any bearing on it.

They were pretty sure that the sound of gunfire had gone off when they were busy sorting the lights and as far as she was aware, Vanic wasn't armed. The sharp pops they'd heard in the distance had chilled her to the core and she had to quickly try to fight off the overwhelming dread that had started to fill her. If something had happened to Van, then they were in serious trouble, and people would likely start looking to her.

Even to her, it seemed like such an obvious trap, but she had to consider that he knew what he was doing. So far, he had gone above and beyond trying to maintain calm and order within the building and it seemed that he must have a lot of experience with this sort of thing. It was surely wasted energy to worry, but it wasn't something she could just switch off and the adrenaline coursing through her body had left her ready to jump to the next problem.

Realistically, the best thing she could do was to make sure everyone here stayed as calm as possible until they had a better idea how that other stuff had played out. If she wanted to show her gratitude to Vanic in particular, she supposed keeping an eye on Noah for him was the best plan of action.

Looking across to the kids it was apparent that the innocence of children was in full effect, and they seemed mostly unfazed by current events. She assumed that to a child, if they had their parents to protect them, there wasn't anything to fear.

Noah in particular was taking things in his stride, and he was busy craning his head about, nose lifted to the air as he made maximum use of his diminutive stature, while taking in his surroundings. She could see a lot of his dad in him, and from the passing comments Vanic had made about his mom, she too sounded like a wonderful parental figure. Melda gleaned from his words that there was in fact a level of intimidation there, as though he thought incurring her wrath was akin to putting the cub of a noble lioness in harm's way.

Her mind betrayed her and she began to picture Noah's face if something happened to his dad. It was heartbreaking and she pushed the idea deep down inside, shaking it off.

The umbral man, she was pretty sure his name was Teorre, having seen his name appear on the staff rota in her office, had taken it upon himself to act as protector and was stood close by Noah's side, hand gently resting on his shoulder.

CHAPTER THIRTY-TWO

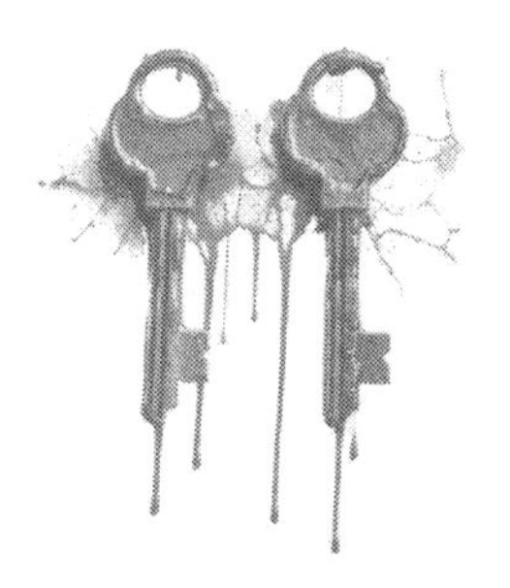

The trio burst into the warehouse, sending the double doors open with an echoing thud as they slammed into the adjoining walls.

Rith wasted no time, dropping to a knee and releasing an arrow at speed towards the first umbral man in the distance. The second umbral, who'd just finished the villainous monologue Rith and the others had been listening to behind the door, was situated behind Vanic and so unfortunately wasn't a viable target.

The arrow caught the man in the right shoulder, sending him to the ground and Jorhim and Karl rushed by on either side, both men charging forth emitting battle cries as they passed.

Vanic, being as reliable as expected, had also sprinted forward, and toppled the other man backwards onto a large pallet crate and was currently locked in battle.

Rith nocked another arrow and waited patiently for an opening in which he could be more help. He could feel the adrenaline coursing through his veins and was surprised at how calm he felt. Surprisingly he was feeling more exhilarated than scared.

The first man was back on his feet immediately and he grabbed the shaft of the arrow in his shoulder, snapping it cleanly off before throwing it to the ground. His eyes burned with a white-hot intensity, and he let out a guttural scream as he rushed forward to meet the two approaching attackers.

Karl and Jorhim closed the gap coming at him from each side in a pincer movement as Jorhim lunged forward swinging the bat with a grunt, putting all his strength behind the swing.

Zavrin twisted to the left and stepped back, watching the bat fly past him at speed, the dwarf's body following through with the swing. Using the momentum of the dodge, he stepped right quickly and lurched forward sending a taloned swipe out at the man in the checked shirt, managing to land only a grazing blow across his chest, tearing his shirt and causing him to emit a short, sharp yelp of pain.

Taking a few steps back, Zavrin brought the hand up to his face and took note of the crimson on his fingertips. With a cruel smile he licked from his palm up to the tip of his index finger and focused his gaze back on the two men.

VANIC LEANED FORWARD DOING HIS BEST TO REMAIN GRAPpled onto Othum as he bucked and twisted violently, trying to free himself from his position compressed beneath him.

He hadn't thought this through before tackling Othum back hard onto the pallet crate. His immediate reaction was to try and incapacitate him as quickly as possible, taking advantage of this new distraction, but right now he found himself in a position less of incapacitation and more of dire struggle, trying to keep Othum's arms pinned. The razor-sharp talons he possessed turned the tussle into a life-or-death situation, much like tackling a man with a knife in each hand while unarmed and Vanic knew that it would take just a second of freedom for him to rend the flesh from his body.

Othum rocked and convulsed beneath him, trying to break free as Vanic used his entire body weight to press down, gripping both his arms at the wrists and maintaining a vicelike grip as he continued struggling for control. They were pressed so close together that it was almost intimate, both bodies grinding against each other as they fought for dominance.

Sweat poured down Vanic's face and he could feel the beads of sweat working their way down his back as they both writhed, locked in combat. He knew that it was only for Othum being pinned awkwardly backwards over the pallet that he was maintaining the upper hand and that it was just a matter of time before the balance shifted and he was in trouble. He could hear the grunts and shouts of combat happening behind him to his left and he hoped that they were faring better in their endeavours.

He could feel the perspiration everywhere now and his grip was beginning to slide, an unwelcome lubrication in his palms arriving at the worst possible time. With a vigorous tug paired with a bucking from Othum's hips, his left hand shifted ever so slightly further up the gripped forearm, and he felt a series of sharp needling pains across the back of his hand as Othum's now tilted wrist clawed at him.

Seizing this momentary break in concentration, Othum leaned in fast and sank his jagged teeth into Vanic's shoulder, burying over a hundred pounds of raw pressure into the bite and tasting the warm metallic tang on his tongue as rich, thick blood ran down his fixed maw.

Vanic howled in pain and struggled to pull himself free from the clutches of the bite, releasing his grip on Othum's right arm and trying to wrench the face away from his shoulder before quickly giving up and jamming his thumb into the eye socket.

Othum reeled in agony releasing the bite as he hissed in pain, jerking his neck to the right and pulling away from the attack. Realising his right arm was now free, he brought his hand up to Vanic's shoulder and buried his fingers into the bite wounds and proceeded to use this momentum to spin them both off the pallet, crashing down hard onto the concrete floor below them.

THE WOODEN BAT CAUGHT ZAVRIN HARD ON THE LEFT THIGH, a blow that would shatter bone on a person afflicted with such things, but to him just succeeded in making him grunt in pain. He turned to focus his attention on the dwarf and rushed forward to close the gap as he raised his arm to deliver a raking slash in retaliation.

Karl threw himself forward and locked onto the arm, gripping it in a bear hug as he wrenched it back. "Again, Jorhim, quickly," he yelled as he tugged the arm, dragging the man back as he hopped to stay upright.

Jorhim stepped forward, the tension heavy in his thigh as he planted his foot and swung again, connecting with the side of the man's torso. The sound it produced and resonating shockwave that ran up his arm was like hitting a tree trunk, dense and muffled.

A cry escaped from Zavrin that was both rage-filled and sonorous and both men felt the cool finger of ice run down their spines, a shiver passing through them as the hairs on their neck stood to attention.

With that building rage and panic running in tandem, Zavrin put all his strength into his throw as he swung Karl around and launched him over his shoulder like a ragdoll into the waiting form of Jorhim, both men clattering to the floor in a heap.

ZAVRIN ROTATED HIS ARM, FEELING THE LINGERING ACHE OF being grappled and readied himself to dive into the scrum and tear them both limb from limb, when another sharp pain hit him.

A second arrow was lodged above his left hip, its black carbon shaft jutting out with its red plastic fletching twinkling up at him as its metallic coating caught the light.

Fuelled with adrenaline he grabbed the shaft, and this time forcefully ripped the whole arrow from his body, black ichor oozing from the wound in his side. He looked up and locked eyes with the elf in the distance, a slanted grin on his face, and began to charge directly at him, arrow raised in hand like a dagger.

A third arrow flew past his right ear as he ran, coming so close he felt the air rush past him and he instantly dodged left as a reaction while he continued to force his legs on, focused on taking down this long-distance threat.

RITH RAGED AT HIMSELF FOR MISSING THAT LAST SHOT, apparently his marksmanship wasn't up to hitting a moving target, and the panic set in as the man was speeding towards him, arm raised high looking to return the arrow he'd just received. With mere seconds to spare he knew there wasn't time to get a second shot off, so he readied the bow at his side to act as an improvised weapon and planted his feet, bent his knees and braced for impact.

FORTUNATELY FOR VANIC THEY'D MANAGED TO MAKE A FULL rotation before hitting the ground, leaving him still on top of the grapple. He had felt the wind knocked out of Othum as they hit the hard concrete and the clawed fingers digging into his shoulder had thankfully released. Not wanting to waste these precious seconds, he brought himself up so that he was sat over the man below him and began to land blow after blow to his face, the impact of each punch rocking his head back into the cold ground below him.

Given the physiology of the umbral people, it was hard to see how much of an effect these blows were having. Midnight black flesh didn't register bruising and so it was just the faint dribbling of a syrupy black liquid from the corners of Othum's mouth that showed any visible signs of damage. Vanic himself had lost more precious fluids as the blood flowed generously from the bite in his shoulder, dripping down onto the man below.

A second wind seemed to invigorate Othum as he again began to buck and thrash his body, wrestling to flip his attacker off him. After a few attempts he managed to free his right arm and brought it up fast, an open palm smashing into Vanic's temple. He followed this impact up with a reflexive twisting of his core, rolling them both and recreating Vanic's former stance. His own strength provided a much more difficult task to shift.

A wicked grin spread across Othum's face, and a sinuous black tongue snaked out to lick at the blood and ichor that was now smeared around his mouth.

"So kind of you to invite your friends to the party," he said, punctuating his statement with a powerful blow to Vanic's Jaw. "They needn't all die for you, but a few more sacrifices to the altar of Vanic can certainly be arranged."

Another obsidian fist crashed into Vanic's face, and he barely managed to roll his neck with the impact, minimising the immediate damage. Having seen firsthand the malicious damage this man's claws were easily capable of, he was aware that the very nature of a closed fist was

Othum's way of toying with him. He was evidently set on prolonging his suffering.

Alongside the pain, he could feel the fresh puffiness of his cheek and the swelling around his left eye was limiting his vision slightly.

He found himself back in his own head once again, fearing for Noah's safety should he fail. A silent apology forced out into the universe to Sarah for failing to keep their son safe, and once again damning himself for not speaking to Roma, for what may have been the final time.

Feeling helpless, he gazed up at the figure above him, the fluorescent light of the ceiling causing a golden shimmer to edge his ebony form. As he stared, the cruel insufferable grin was replaced by a sorrowful dolorous expression, and he tilted his head in mock sympathy.

"Come now Van, where's that fighting spirit? Don't lay down and die on me already." His face twisted back into a sneer as he came down hard with both fists on Vanic's chest, forcing the air out of his body.

"Fight," he said slowly, popping the 't'. "Back."

CHAPTER THIRTY-THREE

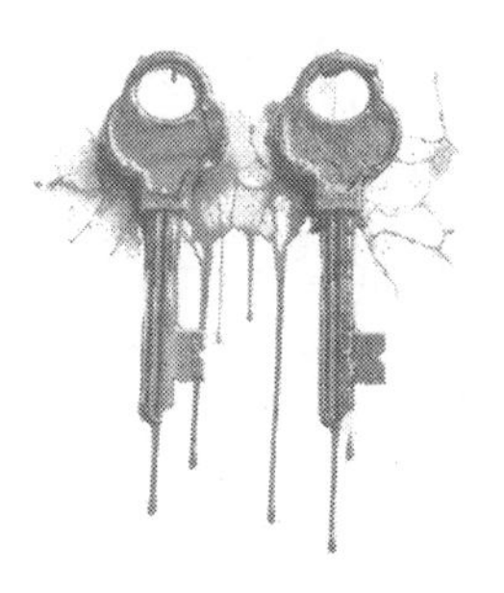

Rith went down hard from the incoming tackle, managing at the last second to swing his bow forcefully into the side of Zavrin's head as he closed in, smashing it painfully into his face but being thrown to the ground regardless. The quiver at his back sent arrows cascading across the ground as he fell with the full weight of Zavrin coming down upon him.

He brought a knee up quickly, connecting with somewhere on his attacker's body as he shoved with both hands against their chest, trying desperately to push him away.

Searing pain flashed across his body as sharp nails dug deep into his arm, tearing through fabric, and finding purchase on his bicep before gripping tightly. He screamed as he tried again to bring up his knee for another blow but lacked the momentum to land any force to the attack.

He could feel the flesh being gouged and torn in the vicelike grip as he tried weakly to knock Zavrin's right arm away as it repeatedly shot at his chest, searching to impale him with the arrow.

Even with his tenacity and determination, it was quickly becoming apparent that he didn't stand much of a chance as he was swiftly being overpowered, the raw, brute strength of the man above him evident and doubly echoed in the look of absolute hatred burning in his eyes.

The realisation of this was now hitting him, and Rith was getting ready to make peace with any of the gods that may or may not exist, when his attackers face took on the stunned countenance of a heavy child discovering he'd misjudged the structural integrity of a high tree branch, and felt his form slide swiftly down his body, the grip on his arm joyously releasing.

He brought himself up on his elbows in time to see Zavrin continue to be dragged backwards, the appearance of Jorhim and Karl each gripping an ankle and pulling him back a sight for sore eyes.

With barely enough time to crack a smile, he witnessed Zavrin jerk his entire body and twist like a crocodile death roll, breaking free of the grip and kicking out with a foot, whipping across Karls's face, and sending him sprawling to the ground.

Zavrin was back on his feet immediately and wasted no time rushing for the sole attacker currently still upright. He let out a shrill, ear-splitting roar as he collided with

Jorhim, digging his nails into the dwarf's left shoulder as he buried the gripped arrow deep into his chest.

Jorhim made barely a grunt as the arrow lodged itself into his body, before bringing both arms, fists clenched, up and out breaking the grip on his shoulder. He followed this up by grabbing his attacker at both shoulders and focused his raw dwarven strength into a powerful head-butt, rocking Zavrin back and obliterating his nose as their skulls collided.

He seized on this opportunity and barrelled into the staggered umbral, using the momentum to drop him to the ground, relishing the satisfying crack as the back of his head connected with the floor.

Karl was back on his feet now and dove to join in the dogpile, swinging heavy fists in tandem with Jorhim, landing blow after blow on the downed man.

Rith scrambled at the floor gathering up his lost arrows as quickly as he could as the two men rained down punches on Zavrin with the intensity of a barroom brawl.

With the sheer ferocity of a man possessed, Zavrin bellowed loudly and managed to cast both men off him like ragdolls flying left and right. He rolled onto Karl and with vicious force, clawed deep into his torso with both hands before ripping away huge strips of flesh with his talons, leaving the exposed ribs underneath visible for a second before waves of blood began to gush from the wounds.

He had only seconds to revel in this small victory before he was sent flying by a well-placed kick from Jorhim, who had recovered his bat and came at him swinging as he struggled to get back on his feet.

Rith rushed to Karl and dropped to a knee, taking in the devastation that had been delivered to his body. A pool of blood was already soaking the ground below him and Karl lay still, his eyes almost black as they stared vacantly at the ceiling above.

"I'm sorry, my friend," Rith said as he reached forward and closed the man's eyes.

Zavrin weaved deftly around the room as Jorhim swung the bat with reckless abandon, trying to land a blow on him. He feinted as the bat swung across him and lashed out with a claw, raking down the dwarf's face, opening up the flesh as blood began to seep from the cuts.

The bat came back around and caught him on the arm, below the elbow sending a shockwave of pain up his body and he felt his fingers go numb. The apparent bloodlust that was now filling the dwarf had increased the strength and speed of his swings and it was starting to become a dangerous situation to be in. He decided to take advantage of the new blind spot caused by the blood running down the man's face and into his eye and shifted round to his right.

He began a series of hit and run attacks as he lunged in, swiping with his claws quickly before stepping back out of the bats range. The blood was now running freely from the dwarf as he had landed six of these swipes across his arms and body, the steam slowly running out of the dwarf's attack as he began to lose blood.

Zavrin was once again looking as if he was in control of the battle, and he grinned menacingly as he started to close in for the kill.

A shrill battle cry out of nowhere threw him, and he turned his head a second too late as the elf flew through the air and came down on him driving an arrow deep into the top of his chest, near his throat.

He staggered backwards as the pain burst from his chest and locked eyes on the man, hatred consuming his thoughts.

"That'll do it," came a deep, hoarse voice as he turned to see the dwarf rushing forward, bat raised high in both hands.

The bat came down on the centre of Zavrin's head and the forceful blow caved in the top of his skull before it snapped sharply to the side, dropping him to the ground.

The bat dropped to the floor with a hollow thunk as Jorhim released his grip and coughed, a small spattering of blood flying from his lips.

"This is why yer don't pick a fight with a dwarf." He dropped to a knee before falling completely back on the ground.

Rith rushed to his side and dragged him under the arms, bringing him to a sitting position up against a metal shelving unit piled high with boxes.

"Just take it easy now, you've done your part." He scrutinised the damage the man had taken in the fight.

"Aye, yer not wrong." He coughed. "Given ma pound of flesh so to speak. Did good yerself too there, elf. Let's hope the man's got his bases covered too, eh?"

Two swift pops of gunfire sounded off from somewhere far away, silencing them both.

CHAPTER THIRTY-FOUR

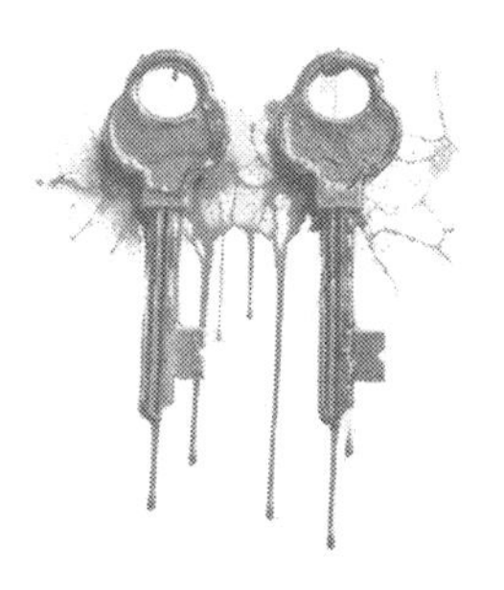

A slap caught Vanic in the cheek causing him to wince, given the damage already done to his face.

The sounds of a brawl could be heard in the distance, and he lay there taking a beating, feebly thrashing his body in an attempt to break free from the attack. People were potentially dying on his watch and the thought of this left a sour taste in him mouth, bile rising in his throat and mingling with blood.

He went limp, relaxing his body for a second hoping this might catch Othum by surprise as he tensed again and jerked his head forward, connecting with his attackers. The results were minimal, but it did cease the flurry of blows that were landing upon him.

"That's better. Show me your fighting spirit," Othum said with a grin.

"Fuck you." Vanic spat. "Let me up and fight me like a man then."

"It's not so easy when you don't have a gun to hide behind is it? Such a wonderful cowardly invention. I'm afraid you're going to have to actually work for it, Van."

Two pistol shots rang out from far away as he thrashed, halting his movement.

"Oh dear," Othum mocked. "I hope your son's ok."

That was it.

Vanic's blood boiled and with a cry he willed every muscle in his body into action, pushing past the waves of nausea that were still coursing through him and thrust up with everything he had, sending Othum tumbling backwards off him.

Both men raised themselves upright simultaneously and Vanic adopted a fighting stance as he braced himself for the coming attack.

"Well, well, well, if that's all the motivation it took, perhaps we should have killed your son ages ago."

"If you have harmed a hair on his head, I swear I..."

Othum cut him off. "What? Kill me? Because I have to say, you're doing a terrible job of that at the moment."

Vanic charged forward in a rage and caught a foot in the stomach for his troubles, doubling him over. Othum followed this up by gripping the back of his head and bringing a knee up, driving it hard into Vanic's face.

The impact staggered him, and he dropped to his knees before losing consciousness.

"Predictable." He sighed as he grabbed Vanic by the collar and started dragging him towards the warehouse doors.

The elf with the bow stood in front of the exit and Othum watched as he considered drawing an arrow, their eyes meeting in a stare, before thinking better of it and turning to flee through the doors.

"Pathetic."

THE SCENE BACK IN THE MALL WAS ALREADY TENSE, WHEN IN the distance, Melda saw Vanic's lifeless form being dragged towards them by an intimidating umbral figure.

Much of the crowd had bolted like scared animals when shots were fired and were now much further down the hall, watching from a safe distance.

Teorre was standing with Noah gripped tightly in front of him, an expression of tense discomfort and unease marring his previous light-hearted demeanour.

Melda, Chuck, and Chrissy were stood across from him, panic and fear plastering each of their faces. A look of resigned failure was apparent.

Chuck's pistol lay on the ground between them.

Though a smattering of others were still close by, they had managed to maintain a small distance from the standoff.

"Everything copacetic?" the man asked, casting a glance to a familiar figure in the crowd.

"Daddy!" Noah cried, losing the composure that he had somehow miraculously held onto until now, tears welling up in his eyes.

"A couple of warning shots, but nothing to be concerned with," Teorre confirmed.

"Fantastic, its wonderful when a plan comes together."

"Whatever this is, can you please just let the child go?" Melda spoke up, maintaining her composure as always. "This has nothing to do with him surely."

"Madam, I can assure you we have no interest in hurting the child, he's just insurance so things will run smoothly," Othum said. "Now, if you could be a delight and kick that gun over to me, please?"

Melda cautiously stepped forward and toed the pistol with her foot, sliding it across the smooth walkway towards Othum as he released his grip on Vanic's collar.

He bent at the knees and rolled Vanic, before slapping him across the face to wake him.

VANIC CAME TO WITH A GASP AND SAT BOLT UPRIGHT, TAKING in his surroundings and the realisation that he'd been moved again. There was an obvious tension in the air and the silence was broken only by the sobbing of a child, a sob he could never misplace. Dread washed over him as he looked to Noah, gripped tightly in the clutches of Teorre. Tears ran down his cheeks and his upper lip bubbled with mucus, shimmering as it reflected the lights above.

He could do nothing but look on in fear, his eyes darting around the hall, piecing together what had happened.

"Glad to have you back with us." The sonorous but mocking tone of Othum filled his ears.

"Now as you can see, Van, there's a gun at your feet. Something you're quite familiar with. In a moment I would like you to pick it up, place it into your mouth and do us all a favour and pull the trigger."

Panicked gasps could be heard from across the hall.

"Should you get any heroic ideas, please know that Teorre here won't hesitate to make that your problem. Or should I say, your son's."

The bastard was enjoying this.

Vanic had never felt so helpless in his entire life, the crushing weight of his failure was flattening him as his stomach churned and the pulsing in his temples clamped like a vice of dread.

"Similarly," he continued. "Should you refuse to do so, rest assured he will find the same fate."

Vanic looked from the trio of worried witnesses to his son, a sight that churned his stomach. Noah had been like a rock this entire time, and to see him reduced to tears was devastating.

"If you would be so kind." Othum gestured towards the pistol laying on the ground.

Vanic reached down and picked up the gun, the stench of gunfire still heavy on the pistol as he brought it up. He surveyed the area around him once more as he weighed up his options.

Basic training drilled into them that you were not to risk taking a shot at a hostage taker as the chance of hitting the hostage was too great. This didn't account for the diminutive stature of a child though and Vanic knew that even with one eye swollen as it was, that he could make that shot with ease.

With Othum at his side, there was no way that was an option. The second he turned the gun onto Teorre,

Othum would be upon him, ruining that opportunity and risking Noah's safety in the process.

He needed to stall things.

"And what happens then? I paint this hall with my blood, and then what?" he said, not taking his eyes off the pistol in his hand.

"Then we're done here," Othum said. "I can't think of a more fitting ending for Vanic the lamplighter, than to meet his demise at his own hands, with the very device created to keep us in subdued."

"And you expect me to believe you'll just let the rest of these people go? And my son?"

"So paranoid to the very end. You have my word. I have no interest in harming anyone else in the building. In fact, perhaps I will see young Noah here in the future, all grown up filled with his father's rage, out for revenge."

He didn't trust a single word that passed through this mad man's lips, but he had exhausted any attempts at buying time and even without any certainty, it was the best chance for the safety of everyone else.

The trauma that witnessing this would cause for Noah filled him with dread but knowing that it was the best way to save his life, he felt no fear. Dying for his son would be as easy at taking a breath.

"Now, if you please." Othum gloated. "We don't have all day."

Vanic raised the gun up towards his mouth.

CHAPTER THIRTY-FIVE

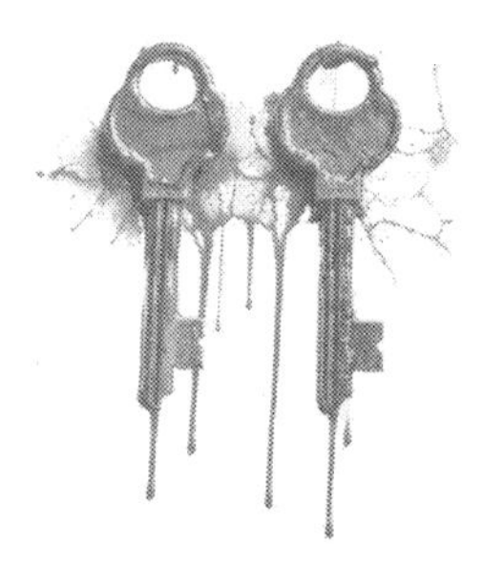

Pandemonium exploded in the hall.

An arrow soared across the walkway and found its mark, hitting Othum in the collarbone, knocking him backwards off his feet.

Vanic spun the gun around without hesitation and fired off two rounds in quick succession.

The first shot flew slightly off target, catching Teorre in the side of the throat, a jet of black liquid spurting from the glancing shot. The second bullet hit home directly above the bridge of his nose, thick black ichor bursting out of the back of his skull as he dropped to the ground.

Melda rushed forward to grab Noah as he bolted from his fallen kidnapper. Van spun on his heels and levelled the gun at Othum, who was slowly standing to his feet. He chanced a quick glance back over his shoulder, up at the balcony of the second floor and saw Rith leaning over the railing, looking worse for wear, bow still in hand.

Focusing his attention back on the man before him, he waited for Othum to look in his direction and squeezed the trigger.

Click.

The magazine was empty.

Flipping the pistol in his grip, he rushed forward to meet Othum and swung the pistol like a club, catching him in the temple, the shock of the blow reverberating up his arm.

Othum staggered backwards and Vanic pressed the attack, catching him again below the jaw and a third time across the forearm as Othum managed to block with his left arm, before rotating and swiping out across Vanic's chest with his right.

The pain was sharp and intense, like being slashed with glass as his flesh opened up and blood trickled from the gashes.

Diving forward, Vanic tackled Othum to the ground and continued to bring the pistol down in clumsy swings as the man thrashed beneath him, landing a few slashes of his own in blind panic, Vanic continued to bleed from the new cuts and scrapes.

Locked in battle, Othum tried wildly to bite at Vanic's face causing him to lurch back, providing Othum with the opening he needed. With all his might, he rolled them and found himself on top of Vanic and began furiously swiping at his face like a man possessed.

With only the pistol for protection, Vanic brought up his arms defensively as he tried to block each blow that came at him and quickly found the flesh on his arms being slashed repeatedly, the blood that poured from them dripping down onto his face.

Like being trapped under a wild dog, panic set in and he continued feebly blocking the onslaught of sharp claws as he heard a thumping sound to his left, moving in their direction.

A tan boot flew over him and caught Othum under the chin as Chrissy kicked with all her might, flipping Othum onto the ground beside him.

The skin on Vanic's arms was shredded and he felt bathed in his own blood. He needed to end this quickly.

Rolling over to sit on Othum's chest he ignored the ferocious swiping claws and snapping of teeth as he once again flipped the pistol and brought it down hard, barrel first at the man's mouth, breaking obsidian teeth as he forced it past his lips.

"Chrissy!" he shouted, praying she would understand.

Without hesitation, she stepped forward and raised one knee before bringing her heel down on the handle of the gun, her powerful leg driving the barrel of the gun through the back of Othum's throat with a sickening crunch.

Vanic stood and watched as Othum's coughing and spluttering slowly turned into a weak gurgle as the life faded from him, a thick tarlike puddle slowly oozing from underneath his skull.

He stumbled towards the nearest storefront to brace himself as his vision began to cloud. Leaning against the window his legs buckled under him, and he slowly slid down the glass finding himself sat, legs splayed out before him as Chrissy rushed over to his aid.

He glanced across the mall to see Noah hugging tightly onto Melda's hip as she wrapped her arm around his shoulders protectively; his crying now abated.

Up on the next level he could just make out the form of Rith, still hanging over the side of the barrier, his right hand up in the air throwing him a thumbs up.

He lifted his own arm, wincing at the pain of the gashes across it, and cast his own thumbs up back at the elf before the world around him faded to black.

CHAPTER THIRTY-SIX

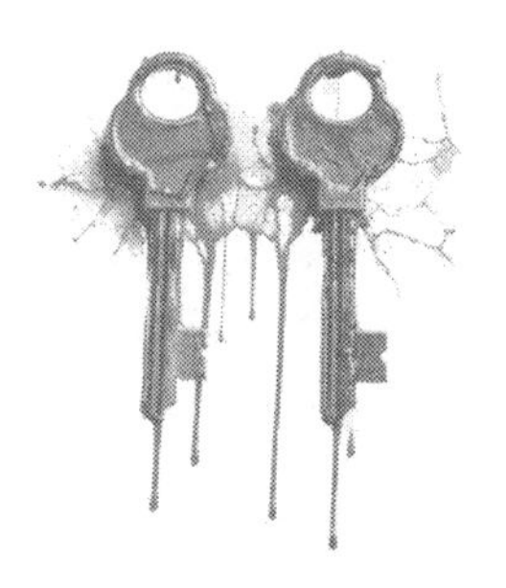

"Just give him a minute."

Vanic tried to open his eyes but the blinding, white lights above burned at his mere slits of vision. He brought his knuckles up to grind the crust out of his eyes with his fingers and felt pain shoot through both hands, which now awakened to consciousness felt raw and painful. Blinking rapidly his Vaseline coated lens of vision began to clean, blurred forms beginning to take shape as spots danced in his eyes.

He focused on the open hands in front of him, knuckles raw and scabbed with dry blood before carrying on up his forearms to see he was wrapped in makeshift bandages, soaked with deep crimson stains. The pain in both arms was a dull, throbbing ache and a heat pulsed within them.

Beyond the end of this makeshift cot, Rith sat on a raised platform, on knee raised as he hugged his arms around it. Behind him a large glass window looked out onto the main walkway of the mall he had considered home this last couple of days. Melda stood to his side, calm as always, a look of concern and worry on her face.

Turning to his left, he saw another cot parallel to his own, a grinning bearded face meeting his.

"Wakey wakey, sunshine." Jorhim's husky voice intoned. "Yer've had all the lasses frettin and fussin over yer here. Save some fer the rest of us, eh?"

"Jorhim?" Vanic said as he tried, painfully to sit up. "Is everyone ok? Where's Noah?" His mind was racing trying to remember the events of the last few hours.

"Noah is fine, rest easy my friend. Though we lost Karl, I'm sorry to say,' Rith chimed in now. 'But other than that, everyone's in one piece. Well, if you can consider what you and Jorhim are, to be one piece."

"And Othum?" Vanic turned his attention to Rith, wincing as he moved.

"Well, your dental skills leave a lot to be desired, but he's out there in a puddle of black sludge. Same for that rat bastard Teorre. You can unclench now; you've been out for the better part of ten hours."

"Ten hours?" He choked on his own outburst.

"Indeed"' Melda said. "We've only come to wake you now as they've just this minute managed to break through the doors. We thought you might want to be up and about for that."

He sat upright and spun his legs, the only parts of him that didn't ache, out of the bed as Melda and Rith both rushed forward to steady him.

"Whoa, hang on there, champ. Let's take things slowly, yeah?" Rith said as he gripped gently on his shoulders.

"Let the lad stretch his bloody legs, he's not made of glass." Jorhim chimed in.

"You're not helping, Jorhim," Melda said as she shot him a disdainful look.

"Yeah, the wife says that a lot," he replied with a grin.

HE WOBBLED ON SHAKY LEGS WITH RITH AND MELDA EITHER side for support as he made his way out into the main body of the mall, every fibre of his being just wanting to hold his son. The crowd had once again gathered in one big group, their focus fixed on the far end of the mall.

Police officers had begun spilling into the building, paramedics on their heels as they made a beeline towards the group. Pistols were readied, but without a sense of urgency and at the front of the pack Vanic could see the chief leading the charge.

Vanic caught his eye and waved casually, wanting to alleviate any immediate concern that might be on his mind. He realised at this point, there had been complete radio silence for some time, and they were still in the dark about what had gone on.

Hot on the heels of the reinforcements, Vanic saw a figure in blue jeans and a lilac tank top, pumping her legs down the hall. He had no doubt in his mind that Sarah had been on the other side of those doors for as long as anyone else. She skidded to a halt and surveyed the area quickly before locking her sights on Noah and rushing to embrace him in a massive hug. He noticed the deep red coloration of the knuckles on her hand. If only he'd had someone here to take that bet on how quickly she'd have punched the first person that stood in her way.

She looked up from her embrace, not relaxing the maternal bearhug one bit, and locked eyes with Vanic giving him a solemn nod that told him he had done well. His head had once again, narrowly avoided her chopping block.

The chief gestured for everyone to relax and made his way towards Vanic.

"Took you long enough," Vanic said as the chief approached.

He eyed Vanic slowly from head to toe and let out a short whistle through his teeth. "Doesn't look like you really needed us. What's the situation?"

"Five dead civilians. Three dead perps and a handful of injured," he said, snapping straight to business.

"Busy couple of days then. Anything else?"

Vanic thought on this for a second.

Where would he begin? The realisation that his best friend was right, and he had harboured a level of unknown prejudice, the fact that he planned to set a reminder on his phone to call Roma every single day for as long as lived, or that even with the unfortunate casualties, he had risen to the task and protected people, like the officer he was destined to be?

"I guess you could say there were some heroics," he said with a smirk.

ACKNOWLEDGMENTS

THIS BOOK, OR WONDERFUL GLOWING E-BOOK, IN YOUR hands is a testament to what you can do when you put your mind to something. Apparently, everyone has a book inside them, you just have to find the time to sit down and let it climb its way up from the fleshy depths you've let it fester in.

It also couldn't exist without other people to serve as wonderful, metaphorical cheerleaders pushing me towards my goal of presenting the finished article.

I would like to thank Jessica Ryn, for taking what I pulled from the grey matter and turning it into the polished work you've just read. Thanks also to Chris for the incredible cover art.

Alongside all the friends that pushed me to finish Umbrate, I would be a true heathen if I didn't also thank my Dungeons and Dragons groups, Sunday book club, and the incredible bookstagram community. You were all way more motivating that you might realise.

And finally, my parents, especially my mother, who sadly didn't get to read this. You planted the seeds for my love of books and watered them as they grew.

ABOUT THE AUTHOR

A.D Jones lives in the North of England, where he spends his time favoring books over people and can be found writing, or devouring said books to review online. He loves Cola, Twin Peaks, cult movies and all things horror. He dislikes the movie *'The Karate Kid'* with a passion that burns brighter than the sun.

You can find him on Instagram
–The_Evergrowing_Library

Printed in Great Britain
by Amazon

29328553R00145